FILTHY RICH CADETS

JILLIAN FROST

YORK MILITARY
ACADEMY

Also by Jillian Frost

Princes of Devil's Creek

Cruel Princes

Vicious Queen

Savage Knights

Cadets of York Military Academy

Filthy Rich Cadets

Very Bad Cadets

For a complete list of books, visit JillianFrost.com.

To my favorite Marine, my dad, for teaching me how to adapt, improvise, and overcome any situation.

FILTHY RICH CADETS

JILLIAN FROST

Cole

Prologue

I would never forget the day Grace came to live with us. She strolled into my home, holding her father's hand. Dressed in a frilly baby blue dress, Grace looked like a porcelain doll with those pink cheeks, big blue eyes that practically jumped off her face, and long, blonde hair that spilled down her back.

I'd never met someone so perfect. I wanted to reach out and touch her, maybe even mess up her hair just to put my mark on her. We were the same age, though she looked much younger. So quiet and shy, she only smiled as my father introduced us.

I brought her hand to my lips and kissed her skin. I'd seen my dad repeat the same motion with my mom, so I figured it was something you did with a girl you liked. She giggled, a blush spreading across her cheeks, then pulled back her hand.

"I'm Colton. But everyone calls me Cole."

Grace toyed with the sleeve of her dress, avoiding my gaze.

1

"You're really pretty," I blurted out.

I learned everything I knew about girls from my dad. Each morning, he told my mom she was beautiful and that he loved her.

John patted her shoulder. "What do you say, Gracie?"

"Thank you," she whispered.

Even at eleven years old, I knew she was important to the Founders. She would grow up thinking the decorated Marine was her biological father. John Hale had sworn an oath to protect Grace because of who she was and what she represented in our world.

For that reason, the Founders chose someone who would risk his life to defend her, a man who could insulate her within the ranks of the United States military, someone our enemies would least suspect. As long as John lived, Grace wasn't in danger.

"Do you like movies?"

Grace pressed her lips together, then nodded.

I offered her my hand. "Wanna watch one with me?"

She shrugged, indifferent. But in my young mind, it was like asking a girl out and having her say yes. I knew I couldn't keep her—because the Founders would never allow it. But I was a selfish bastard who hated the word no.

John tapped her on the back. "Go ahead, Gracie. I have some business to discuss with your uncle Mark."

I took one last look at our parents before dragging her out of the living room, leading her down the main hallway. Grace's hand was tiny compared to mine. She was like a doll. So precious and perfect, a little thing I didn't want anyone else to touch.

She was mine.

As we walked through the house, her hand trembled, shaking through me.

I glanced over at her. "You don't have to fear me. I won't hurt you."

She'd been through hell in her short life, and I wondered if she remembered what her life was like before the Founders appointed John Hale as her guardian. Did she know her real name or recall anything about her past? For her sake, I hoped she only had memories of her adoptive father and the future she could have now that she was part of our world.

We stepped into a room at the back of the house with movie theater seating and a concession stand. I slid behind the counter and grabbed the box of kernels.

"Cole," she said in a soft tone that made every hair on my arms stand at attention. "Do you have Captain America?"

I was so surprised by her question I almost laughed. "Yeah, we have it. You like Cap?"

She bobbed her head, and her hair fell in front of her blue eyes. "He reminds me of my dad."

If you only knew the truth, I wanted to say. *Your real dad would scare the monsters under your bed.*

After preparing the popcorn, I sat beside Grace in the front row with the bowl in my lap. We stuffed popcorn into our mouths and watched the first Captain America movie. Grace's eyes didn't leave the screen, though a few times, I caught her looking at me from the corner of her eye. My heart pounded every time I sensed her searching for me.

Midway through the movie, we finished the popcorn. I set the bowl on my left, then moved my right hand between us. As if she felt the same tug that drew me to her, she inched her fingers closer to mine.

For the last ten minutes of the movie, we held hands. It was a simple gesture, nothing special. That was the start of our friendship.

Every summer from that day forward, Grace lived at Fort Marshall with my family. All year, I looked forward to the three months we spent together, desperate to finish school so I could see her again. But, as we got older, our relationship slowly entered the forbidden territory.

The Founders would have killed me, but I didn't care. Because Grace was worth the risk.

Grace

Ten years later

I could sense *them* from a distance. My cadets were always watching, waiting for me. If I turned my head, I would find Cole and Hunter staring at me from across the pool.

It was dark that night, the enclosed pool house dimly lit by lanterns to hide the debauchery taking place at the party. I staggered past a row of tables with my cell phone clutched in my hand, fighting the tears that threatened to spill from my eyes.

Loud music blared through the speakers, assaulting my eardrums. I swiped a bottle of vodka from a table. A man groaned and then yelled for me to give it back.

I raised the bottle to my lips and took a big gulp, closing my eyes as the alcohol slid down my throat.

It felt good.

The burn.

Dozens of Cole's friends surrounded me. I'd met them over the years at parties, but I couldn't remember most of their names. Some guys attended York Military Academy with Cole and his younger brothers. The girls went to Ivy League colleges and were home for the summer break.

Everyone in town wanted an invitation to Fort Marshall, a sprawling estate on Founders Way. The Marshalls were richer than gods and known for their over-the-top parties.

My father came from humble beginnings and never spoiled me. Even with his high rank and substantial salary from the Marine Corps, we still lived a frugal life. And since I'd never met my mother, it was just the two of us.

I'd grown accustomed to the lack of luxury. But every time I stepped inside Fort Marshall, I wanted to be one of them. One of the elite. I wondered what it would be like to have so much wealth.

Would I grow bored with it?

Would I only want more?

I'd never spent enough time at Fort Marshall to find out. For ten years straight, I lived with the Marshalls for the summer break, long enough to get a taste of their lifestyle without being spoiled by it.

"Hey, beautiful," Rhys Vanderbilt said in my ear. "Where are you going?"

When I ignored him, he tugged on my bikini strap. I turned to my left, irritated when my eyes landed on the tall, black-haired boy with straight teeth and a mischievous smile.

He was in the same platoon as Cole and Hunter at the academy. Rhys was devilishly handsome and filthy rich. He was used to getting whatever he wanted, a spoiled brat to the core.

Shooting him a nasty look, I swatted his hand away. "Take a hint, Rhys."

He breathed vodka in my face. "You're just mad because Preston is cheating on you with Cecelia."

"I don't give a damn," I lied, holding back the wave of emotions sweeping over me. "He can fuck whoever he wants. We're not together anymore."

Less than one hour ago, I caught my now ex-boyfriend fucking a mystery woman. I didn't know her name was Cecelia, nor did I care. And now that I could put a name to the face, I was even angrier.

I could almost hear him calling out her name as he bent the nasty bitch over his desk and fucked her from behind. She screamed like a porn star, too, which made it a hell of a lot worse—because Preston wasn't that good in bed. Not to get that kind of applause from his whore.

Cole had introduced me to Preston Carter. The rich dick I thought would be my saving grace until I told him about my father's new duty station.

Of course, I agreed to follow my dad because that was how we operated. I was old enough to make my own decisions and live my own life. But I'd made a promise to stick with my dad until he retired from the Marine Corps.

Rhys yanked on my arm, manhandling me once more. With quick reflexes, I grabbed his arm and twisted it behind his back, a move my dad had shown me. He had insisted I learn martial arts for self-defense.

Rhys reached behind his back, his fingers digging into my skin. "Let me go, bitch."

I tightened my grip. "Say the magic words."

He turned to the left and tapped on my arm. "You're fair game now. Preston doesn't want you, but that doesn't mean we can't be friends, Grace."

My little show had garnered some attention from the partygoers. Dozens of eyes watched me as Rhys squirmed and yelled for me to let him go. And since he was boring me, and I wasn't here to watch him piss himself, I released him from my death grip.

"I think I'll pass," I told him. "I'm not into pretty boys."

He snickered. "What do you call Preston?"

I shrugged. "Don't care. He's dead to me."

Rhys raised his hands and backed up. "I don't want any trouble, okay? I was messing around."

Confused, I narrowed my eyes at him.

I spun around and found Cole and Hunter blocking my path like a wall of hard muscle. They glared at the idiot behind me and then refocused their intense expressions on me.

I pulled out my cell phone and flipped to the video I'd taken of Preston and Cecelia. Neither of them had heard me in the doorway. So I filmed a video as proof so the bastard couldn't lie about his affair. He was recording them with a camera set up in the room's corner, so I figured why not?

I wanted revenge for what he did to me.

Cole and Hunter were the perfect escape from reality. They would make me forget, which was why I raced over to Fort Marshall the second I hit Stop on the video.

I held out my phone, and Cole took it from my hand. He invaded my space, his warm, hard body pressed against my chest. A chill rolled down my arms as I looked up at him. Even as kids, one look from Cole always made my heart pound.

"I want Preston to pay."

I should have known Preston would move on after I told him about my father's promotion. He said we could make long-distance work, but that was a lie. Military brats never lived in one place for more than a few years. We learned how to adapt and improvise to our current situation because how else do you survive the constant change?

It was impossible to make long-term friends or have a boyfriend. Every relationship, much like my father's duty station, had an expiration. But that didn't make Preston's betrayal hurt any less.

At least Cole was here.

He was my first real friend.

Cole knew all of my secrets.

His eyes fell to the screen, teeth clenched as he watched the video. He had white-blond hair cut short on the sides and longer on the top with rugged features that made him less of a pretty boy. But he was still pretty, with long black eyelashes that made me a little jealous, and those piercing blue eyes that reminded me of sapphires.

Hunter shoved a hand through his dark hair and watched the video over Cole's shoulder. He was taller than Cole and had more muscle, his arms thick like a professional athlete. Years of training at a military academy had given both of my cadets perfect bodies I often thought about when we were apart. I only got to see them over the summer and on the occasional holiday during the school year. It had been too long since I last had them all to myself.

"We said we would never repeat what we did last year. But I need you, Cole." My gaze shifted to Hunter. "I need both of you."

"My little brat," Cole groaned. "You're not like us. You don't want to do this again."

While I didn't love being a military brat, I loved it when he called me *his* brat.

"Yes, I am." I licked my lips. "I want this. Don't make me beg."

He threaded his fingers between mine. The sudden contact tingled my skin with excitement. Cole knew how to make me forget, how to take away my pain.

"I'd like to see you beg," Hunter said against the shell of my ear. The combination of his words and the heat from his breath made me shiver. "On your knees. Bent over the bed, face down, ass up. With Cole's cock in your mouth while I lick your pussy. You want that?"

I nodded.

I wanted all of it.

Hunter sucked my earlobe into his mouth, and I fell back against his chest. "You going to beg for me, baby girl?"

I moaned, excited by the promise.

My nipples hardened into peaks that poked through the thin fabric of my bikini top. With a few dirty words, he drenched my bottoms, and my pussy clenched from the magic Hunter and Cole worked between my thighs.

Between the two of them, I could never get enough. They made me do crazy things I'd never considered before we got drunk one night and ended up in bed.

Cole led me by the hand through the crowded house with Hunter on my rear. He loved the view, taking every opportunity to touch my ass as we ascended the stairs. Once we reached the top landing, Hunter dug his fingers into my hip, pulling me into his side. He was several inches taller than Cole's six feet, but both of them towered over me.

Once inside Cole's bedroom, Hunter hooked his arms around me, pinning my back against his chest.

Cole slid his fingers beneath my chin. "Are you sure you want this?"

"I want revenge."

"How do you plan to get it?"

I held up my phone. "By sending every dirty deed to Preston. Karma is a bitch."

An evil grin stretched the corners of Cole's beautiful mouth.

I knew it would kill Preston.

His ego couldn't handle the blow.

Preston attended York Military Academy with Cole and Hunter and competed with them at everything. The highest grades, top marksmanship, literally anything that had a clear winner. I'd always wondered if he only chased after me to get under Cole's skin.

Because he knew I was important to him. And now, Cole and Hunter would get to rub our night together in his smug, entitled face.

Grace

After I set up the camera and hit Play, I didn't feel an ounce of regret. It was more than sex with Hunter and Cole. There were gaps in my memories, chunks of my life missing from my brain.

Parts of my childhood didn't exist, as if my life hadn't started until I walked into Fort Marshall ten years ago. Some of my happiest memories were with Cole. The boy who welcomed me into his world and made me feel like I finally belonged somewhere.

Then Hunter came along.

He was charming and handsome, and I had difficulty resisting the urge to hold his hand when he offered it to me. Hunter Banks was the son of a weapons manufacturer. His family did business with the Marshalls. They were like brothers, and when I was with them, I felt at home.

I pressed my ass against Hunter's hard cock, which earned me a groan in response. Hunter bit my ear and rocked his hips, releasing one of my arms so he could tug at the strings of my bikini bottoms, unfastening each side until the fabric dropped to the floor.

13

Cole licked his lips and rested his forehead against mine as his hand slipped between my legs. "She's so wet," he said to Hunter. "You gonna cum for me, brat?" He slid his finger inside me, and I cried out from the sudden contact. He drew back and added another finger.

"You gonna cum all over my cock, baby girl?" Hunter growled in my ear.

"Yes."

My eyes slammed shut from the intense waves of pleasure that rolled down my arms. I reached behind me to hook my arms around Hunter's neck, and Cole dropped to his knees in front of me, staring up at me as he continued to thrust his fingers. Hunter lifted me as Cole threw my legs over his shoulders. He was so close to my throbbing pussy, the heat from his breath sent chills down my legs.

When Cole's tongue glided over my aching clit, every part of my body heated from the inferno only my cadets could extinguish. Hunter slid his hand beneath my chin and turned my head until our eyes met. His lips crashed into mine, his tongue slipping into my mouth. He kissed me like I just stole his last breath, and he wanted it back, consuming me with each flick of his tongue.

As Cole licked my pussy, Hunter kissed his way down my neck and massaged my nipples. My legs shook uncontrollably as my orgasm rocked through me, forcing Cole to hold me in place as his tongue darted in and out of me. Hunter captured each of my moans with his mouth, making me dizzy with lust and hungry for more. I exploded on Cole's tongue, coming so fucking hard my entire body felt numb.

Cole dropped my legs to the floor and licked my juices from his lips. His blue eyes were electric, fueled by desire, as he pressed his lips to mine. "Let Hunter taste you," he said, breathless.

My heart thumped, slamming into my chest, begging to break free. What difference did it make if we made one last crazy decision? We'd made plenty of them before that night.

When we were sixteen, Cole took my virginity on the cabana bed by his pool. I gave him everything—my heart included. It wasn't until years later that I let Hunter join us.

Cole raised his shirt over his head, exposing his rock-hard abs that made my mouth water. He looked like a boy who grew up at a military academy, and now he was a man with a body chiseled to perfection. Hunter was bigger than Cole with solid shoulders and thick biceps corded with muscle.

Cole looked like the All-American boy, while Hunter reminded me of a sailor with the dark ink on his arms and chest. They both had the same tattoo on their right bicep—a gladiator helmet with wings and two crossed swords. They said it had to do with the academy and their brotherly bond.

I bit my bottom lip as Cole pushed his shorts over his hips, and his long, hard cock sprang free. He took my hand and led me to his king-sized bed. I dropped to the floor between his thighs, and he wrapped his big hand around his shaft, giving himself a few strokes. Precum slid down his skin, and he used it to wet his cock, staring at my mouth to communicate what he wanted from me.

Hunter undressed behind me, and then he ripped open a foil packet. He lifted me from the floor, and with his palm on my lower back, Hunter bent me over, forcing me to grab Cole's thighs to maintain my balance. Cole shoved the hair out of my face, pushing it behind my ears so he could look at me.

Fisting Cole's cock in my hand, I licked the cum from his skin, rolling my tongue in a circular motion that drove him crazy. My cheeks puffed out as he fucked my mouth, practically choking me. I tapped his thigh, and Cole loosened his grip on my hair, making it easier for me to take as much of him as I could fit.

Hunter lined himself up at my entrance from behind, kneading my breast as he slammed into me, tearing through my inner walls. Much like Cole, Hunter was never careful with me. Neither of them treated me like I was breakable.

"Fuck, baby girl," Hunter said as he pounded into me. "Your pussy is so tight."

He stretched me out as I took more of Cole, whose legs were shaking. I could tell he was close, ready to ride his high along with Hunter. But Cole was also selfish with me. If Hunter got to fuck me, then Cole wanted to make me come twice as hard.

Hunter moved his hand to my ass and pressed his thumb between my cheeks, applying enough pressure to hit the spot. "I want to fuck your tight ass while Cole stretches out your pussy."

I moaned with Cole's cock in my mouth. Hunter leaned forward, sweat sliding down his chest and onto my back. He could go for hours if he wanted to make it last all night. So could Cole. After some of our nights together, I couldn't even get out of bed for an entire day. They were the perfect duo and my biggest weakness.

Cole grabbed the back of my head, and his cock popped out of my mouth. Our eyes met for a split second before Hunter slid out of my pussy, making me instantly feel the loss between my legs. He threw a condom onto the bed next to Cole.

Cole rolled it on and gave me a look that said, *Come here.* He laid back on the bed, and I climbed on top of him, slowly sliding down his length as I took every inch of him. He gripped my hips and thrust deeper and deeper.

Hunter grabbed a bottle from Cole's dresser and lubricated my entrance, plunging his finger into my ass. Chills rolled down my arms as a wave of pleasure commanded control of my body.

"I want to fuck all of your holes." Hunter replaced his finger with the tip of his cock. "Damn, baby girl. Fuck, you feel so good."

Hunter was so big that I sucked in a deep breath as he slowly inched his way inside me. Hunter straddled Cole's thighs, repositioning himself as he prepared me for his size. I could tell when Cole felt Hunter's cock push against his because his eyes widened.

Cole and Hunter never touched.

It was always about me.

I was their sole focus.

Pleasing me. Teasing me.

Making me come.

Begging them for more.

A smile tugged at my mouth. Then Cole's lips crashed against mine, the taste of expensive whiskey and cloves penetrating my senses. He only smoked at parties when he was drinking and home from the academy. Both Cole and Hunter's lives revolved around their future military careers. They loved their fellow cadets like brothers. And, if anyone understood their lifestyle, it was me.

That was why this worked between us.

We all knew what to expect.

Nothing in our world was permanent.

Our bodies worked in unison, each of our brewing orgasms shaking through our connection. As Hunter groaned my name, Cole muttered curses under his breath. Hunter came first and then pulled out of me, giving me a few more seconds with Cole, who thrust into me right before he came inside me.

Hunter kissed the top of my head and tapped my ass. "I missed you, baby girl. I'm glad you ditched that loser boyfriend."

More like he ditched me.

"When do you leave for Virginia?" Cole asked with the same sadness that was always present in his eyes.

"Tomorrow afternoon."

He slid his thumb across my bottom lip. "Then I guess we better make you cum a few more times before you go."

Cole would never tell me he missed me, but I knew he did. He loved me in his fucked-up way. They both did. I didn't expect anyone to understand my relationship with them.

"Don't forget to send the video to Preston."

Cole grinned. "He's going to lose his shit."

"He deserves worse."

Hunter wrapped his fingers around my throat and tilted my head back until our eyes met. "I love your evil side, baby girl. It's such a turn-on."

"I'm not done with you, brat." Cole jerked his hard cock. "My soldier's standing at attention for you."

Hunter brushed his lips against my earlobe. "And baby, we salute you."

Grace

My dad stumbled in from work an hour late, a worried expression tugging at his dark features. He looked as if he'd aged months since I saw him that morning over breakfast.

I could see the frustration on his face as he scrubbed a hand over his jaw. He dropped his keys on the entrance table, then his gaze swept across the room to me.

"I wasn't sure if I should eat without you." I leaned forward on the couch, my elbows on my thighs. "You're never late."

My dad valued punctuality, a quality he had instilled in me. As a result, I was never late for anything, ever.

He pressed his lips into a thin line. "What did you make?"

"Nothing special. Steak and potatoes on the grill."

Dad forced a grin. It was his favorite food, so why did he look so miserable?

Still dressed in his uniform, he walked toward the couch, with Sarge prancing like a good pup at his side.

He'd gotten me the English bulldog for my eighteenth birthday to keep me company while he was away on an extended mission.

He sat on the couch beside me and squeezed my knee. "Gracie, I have some bad news."

That was the last thing I wanted to hear after moving for the ninth time. I was trying to put down some roots and make Virginia Beach my home. Bad news usually meant one of two things—we were moving again, or he was leaving me behind.

"What's wrong, Dad?"

Eyes downcast, he sighed. "Willow Marshall died."

I gasped at his confession. "What happened to her?"

"She committed suicide."

"But…" I struggled to find the correct words because my heart was beating too fast for me to catch my breath. "She was so happy." I shook my head, confused. "Willow wouldn't kill herself."

He peeked up at me from beneath his dark brows. "All the signs point to suicide. Mark is waiting for the medical examiner to determine the exact cause of death. She slit her wrists and then jumped into the pool. Cole found her body."

Tears dripped from my eyes, spilling down my cheeks. "Cole found his mom?"

He nodded. "Mark had to drain the pool of her blood."

"When is the funeral? We have to go."

"It was last night."

"What? Why didn't you tell me sooner? I want to say goodbye to Willow."

"I'm sorry, Gracie. Unfortunately, it's too late."

I rubbed my eyes and choked out, "How is Cole doing?"

"Not good," he admitted with a severeness to his tone. "Mark said Cole hasn't spoken to anyone since he found her. He sits in his room and stares at the wall."

My heart ached for him. Cole had always been my rock, and I wanted to comfort my best friend.

"How are the boys? And Mark?"

Cole had two younger twin brothers, Knox and Sloan, who were in their last year of high school at York Military Academy.

"Mark is trying to be strong for his sons. But he's not okay." Dad let out a deep breath, tightening his grip on my hand. "I can't imagine what he's going through. If I were to lose you... You're all I've got."

"You don't have to worry about losing me. I'm not going anywhere."

A frown tugged at his mouth. "I worry every single day, Gracie. What I do for a living is dangerous. I've made certain decisions in my life, and I can't walk away."

"What are you talking about?"

"I have more bad news." He lifted my hand from

the couch and held it in his hand like he was afraid to let me go. "I have to leave tomorrow night for a special mission."

I wiped the tears away, though they wouldn't stop coming. "No, you can't leave. We just got here."

He moved his hand to my shoulder and pulled me into a one-arm hug. "I don't have a choice. Duty calls. I'll be back in three months."

I frowned. "You promised this time would be different. One more duty station and then retirement."

"I intend to keep that promise. I'll be home before you know it. Sarge will keep you company." He ran his hand down her back, and Sarge leaned into my dad. "Isn't that right, girl? You'll take care of Gracie for me while I'm gone."

Sarge licked his hand in response.

"What kind of mission?" I asked.

"You know that's classified."

"Can you at least tell me where?"

He shook his head. "I'll call you every Sunday. So unless you stop hearing from me, you have nothing to worry about, kiddo."

The thought of him missing a check-in made my stomach ache. He was the only family I had left, not including the Marshalls. They had been my pseudo-family since I was a kid.

"Why does this feel more permanent than last time?" I asked him with tears in my eyes.

"There are four things I value most in this world, Gracie. Duty, honor, country, and family. I try to put you first. You are my number one priority. But you're an adult now and can handle yourself. I like to think I taught you well."

"You did. I've learned to adapt to any situation because of you. It doesn't make this suck less each time we say goodbye."

Dad flipped over my hand and traced an infinity symbol on my palm with his index finger. He did this every time he left. This was our version of always and forever.

Because family is forever.

"I love you, Dad," I whispered between sobs. "Just come back to me in one piece. Don't forget to call."

"Love you, too." He kissed my forehead. "I never do. Every Sunday, same as always."

He fell back on the couch when Sarge jumped onto his lap, licking his face. My dad hugged her around the middle like she was his second child and rubbed behind her ears. Sarge laid her head on my dad's chest and soaked up his love and attention.

I fished my cell phone from my pocket and scrolled to Cole's name.

Why didn't he tell me about Willow?

We told each other everything and had no secrets between us. Maybe he was too busy helping his father plan her funeral. Or maybe he was still in shock.

My chest felt as if it were ready to collapse from breathing so hard, wishing I could be there to comfort Cole during the worst moment of his life.

Dad tapped my leg, then shot up from the couch. "I have to pack. Take Sarge for a walk, and then we'll have dinner together."

Our last dinner for months.

I smiled, even though it hurt like hell to contain my emotions. "Yeah, sounds good, Dad."

As he walked into his bedroom, I attached Sarge's leash to her collar and took her outside. A mixture of purplish-blue hues swept across the horizon. We were so close to the Atlantic Ocean I could smell the saltiness of the sea in the air. I breathed it in and let it wash over me like breaking waves.

I missed Cole and Hunter.

But I missed Cole most of all.

I clutched my phone, thinking about what I would say to Cole, and drew a blank. When my grandmother died, it hurt like hell. Cole had held me in his arms while I cried and kissed me until I fell back to sleep. I considered driving to Devil's Creek to tell him that everything would be okay.

But would it?

I'd never lost a parent.

My mother was never in my life.

She was a German woman my father met while stationed at Ramstein Air Base. He said she wanted nothing to do with me and handed me to my dad right after she'd given birth.

What kind of mom does that?

Sarge dragged me down the block, headed toward the ballpark, where some guys played softball after work. I stopped walking when we reached the fence, which lined the perimeter, and finally mustered enough courage to make the call. The line rang once before it went straight to voicemail.

That's weird.

I figured he had terrible reception because Cole never ignored my calls. So I tried him again and got his voicemail right away.

I looked down at Sarge, who peeked up at me with her cute puppy face. "I know Cole isn't ignoring me."

Why was I talking to the dog like she could give me advice about Cole?

Frustrated, I dialed Hunter, knowing he would give me some answers, and got his voicemail after the first ring.

What the fuck is wrong with them?

Determined to reach one of them, I hit redial. The phone rang once before Hunter sent me to voicemail.

"Okay, what the fuck is going on?" I mumbled, and Sarge jumped up on me as if she could sense I needed a hug.

Devil's Creek was a nine-hour drive from Virginia Beach, and I had college classes at eight o'clock in the morning. I didn't have time to drive there and back, so I sent Hunter a text message.

Grace: I just heard about Willow. I keep getting voicemail. How is Cole?

I waited ten minutes before I received a response.

Hunter: Not good. You shouldn't call him.
Grace: Why not?
Hunter: He doesn't need you.
Grace: I want to be there for him.
Hunter: He doesn't want you, Grace.

My heart sank to my stomach. At least Hunter had the decency to answer me, but he wasn't acting like himself. He was usually so sweet, always trying to charm his way into my pants.

Grace: How about you? How are you holding up?

No response.

Grace: Talk to me, Hunter. Don't shut me out.

Twenty minutes passed before my phone dinged again.

Cole: Lose my fucking number. And while you're at it, forget Hunter's.

With those words, he ripped a hole in my heart the size of the Grand Canyon. I never thought I would feel pain like that again, but I was so wrong. Because the worst day of my life had yet to come.

Cole

I hit send and threw my cell phone across the room. The screen hit the wall and crashed onto the hardwood floor. I could buy another phone, but I couldn't replace *her*. I hated myself for pushing Grace away, but it was the right thing to do.

"Are you sure about this?" Hunter kicked his boot up on the ottoman, a cold beer in his hand. "Grace is going to lose her mind without us."

"We don't have a choice, Hunter." I sipped scotch straight from the bottle, reveling in the burn as the liquor slid down my throat. "Those bastards killed my mom and made it look like she committed suicide. Grace has to stay away from us."

The Founders tasked my family with keeping Grace safe from her enemies. I was not allowed to touch her, but she was too pretty and perfect, too fucking mine. From the moment we met, I knew I would have her. But to keep her safe, she had to hate me.

"If they find Grace, they will kill her, too."

Hunter downed the rest of his beer and slammed

the bottle down on the table. "Have you considered she might be safer with us?"

I shook my head. "No, she's better off with John Hale."

"The Colonel is leaving tomorrow for his final mission," he said in a pained tone. "There's a chance he won't come back."

I looked up from the bottle in my hand. We had been through a lot of shit together. Cadet training at York Military Academy and years of pushing ourselves to the limits before being initiated into The Devil's Knights.

Secret societies governed our world, and we were members of one of the highest-ranking organizations in the United States. The Founders Society ran the country, controlled the financial system, and had even infiltrated the military. We had everyone from politicians to bankers in our pockets. There was nothing out of our reach. Not until the Knights had gotten mixed up with The Lucaya Group.

I'd spent my entire life preparing for battle, except this wasn't the war I had expected. Our enemies were stronger, more powerful, and always ten steps ahead. I wanted revenge so badly for my mother's death I couldn't think straight, which why Grace had to stay in Virginia Beach. It was the reason my father didn't want Grace and her dad traveling to Devil's Creek for the funeral.

She was better off anywhere but here.

"They killed my mom," I said again, hoping it would sink into Hunter's thick skull. "Grace is never coming back to Devil's Creek. Do you understand me? I won't have her blood on my hands."

He nodded in agreement.

Grace

I sat in the campus cafeteria beside my new friend and shoved a turkey sandwich into my mouth. My cell phone rang, cutting through the noise in the crowded room.

It was a local number I didn't recognize, so I rejected the call. We had thirty minutes before our next class and needed to hurry and eat before we had to rush across campus.

"Who's that?" Veronica asked between bites.

"No one I know."

The same number called back.

"Ugh, if this is another annoying telemarketer."

"You haven't heard from your dad in a while," she pointed out.

I'd been counting down the seconds since our last call. The time usually ran through my mind all day on repeat, but over the past hour, I tried to forget. My curiosity wouldn't allow me to send the caller to voicemail again, so I raised the phone to my ear and said hello.

"Grace Hale," a woman said, and my heart

skipped a beat. "I work for Dean Perkins. He needs to meet with you right now. It's urgent."

Hands trembling, I dropped the rest of my sandwich onto the plate, the food churning in my stomach. "Sure, I can come now. Do you know what this is about?"

"He'd like to discuss the matter with you in person."

"Okay. I'll be there in a few minutes."

"See you soon," she said before ending the call.

I stuffed the phone into my backpack and glanced over at Veronica. "That was weird. Dean Perkins wants to see me."

"What did you do?"

"I don't know."

I hadn't heard from my dad in weeks, which wasn't like him. He missed our last two Sunday phone calls.

Veronica slung her bag over her shoulder and slid off the bench with the tray in hand. "I'll walk you to Perkins' office."

We navigated the campus in near silence. My stomach twisted into knots when we walked into the administrative building, nausea sweeping over me with each step closer to the dean's office.

Veronica slipped her fingers between mine. "I'm sure it's nothing. Students get called to the dean's office all the time."

I raised an eyebrow at her. "Do they? Because this is a first for me."

I squeezed her hand for dear life. Only someone in my position could understand the constant fear I felt daily. For years, I had mentally prepared myself for the potentially bad news. That was the reason I begged my dad to retire. The worrying and waiting around made me sick to my stomach.

Veronica patted my bicep and sighed. "Don't worry over nothing."

"No news is good news. My dad says that before every deployment. But he's never missed our Sunday phone calls."

She opened her mouth to speak and quickly snapped it shut. We stopped outside of Dean Perkins' office, and Veronica hugged me.

"Come find me afterward."

Digging my teeth into my bottom lip, I nodded.

Veronica walked in the opposite direction, her skirt swaying with each shake of her hips, and then she disappeared around the corner.

I took a deep breath and entered the waiting area. Sitting behind a long oak desk, Dean Perkins' secretary switched between multiple lines, informing the callers to hold.

"I'm Grace Hale."

Her eyes widened, and then she shifted the phone to her shoulder. "They're waiting for you. Go ahead."

She tipped her head toward the open the door to the left of her desk. I froze in the doorway when my eyes landed on Mark Marshall, my godfather and my father's best friend. He sat in the chair across from the dean. Tears burned my eyes, but I fought to keep them at bay until I heard the words from his mouth.

Dad is okay.

He has to be okay.

Consumed by fear, I swallowed the lump forming at the back of my throat. This was terrible news. I could feel it in my bones as I walked into the room. Mark's eyes were glassy, his shoulders slumped against the leather chair.

Dean Perkins noticed me first and stood, buttoning his suit jacket as his eyes met mine. "Grace, take a seat." He lifted a box of tissues from the desk as he stepped out from behind it.

"What's going on?" I could barely get out the words. "Is my dad okay?"

Mark was on his feet, his blue eyes red-rimmed. He stood tall, well over six feet, and dressed in a navy jacket and pants with white stripes down the sides of the legs. Every cadet at York Military Academy wore the same uniform.

As usual, not a single hair was out of place. His black waves were cut so short you couldn't tell he had naturally curly hair. Mark looked as if he was doing everything in his power to hold it together, while on the verge of falling apart. The muscles in his face twitched as he fought to maintain his stony expression.

"Gracie." Mark wrapped his arms around me, towering over me as he rested his chin on the top of my head. He cleared his throat. And now I knew for sure that my initial suspicions were correct. "Your dad…"

"Don't say it." I clutched his arm tighter, digging my fingers into his thick jacket. Tears spilled down my cheeks and soaked my shirt. "I don't want to hear you say it."

"He didn't suffer."

For the first time, Mark cried in front of me. His tough-guy facade crumbled with each painstaking breath he took. I collapsed in his arms, and he cradled me against his chest, my tears bleeding through his dress shirt.

Mark palmed the back of my head. "I swore to your dad, and before God, I would protect you if anything were to happen to him."

"What happens now?" I said between sobs.

"You'll come home with me."

"I can take care of myself. I've been doing it my whole life."

"I know you can, Gracie." He clutched my shoulder. "But you're only a kid."

"I'm twenty-one, not a child."

"You have no money and nowhere to go. Come home with me until we figure something out."

There was no point in arguing with Mark. I had no one and nothing other than a few hundred bucks in my checking account. Because we moved so much, my dad never put down roots anywhere. We never had a permanent home.

"Do you know what happened to him?"

"I should have been there. If I had, maybe the situation would have turned out differently."

Mark and my dad were in the same unit before his discharge.

"If you were with him, you might be dead, too."

Then I would have no one.

"My boys already lost one parent."

After my night with Cole and Hunter, everything changed. Cole's mom committed suicide, and then he told me to stop contacting them. That was all I got from Cole after years of friendship. He was hurting on the inside, and he wanted to take out his frustration on someone.

That person was me.

I tried to put Cole and Hunter in the rearview mirror. But now, there was no escaping him. I was about to become his roommate.

I took a few steps back and attempted to gather myself, wiping tears from my cheeks with the back of my hand. Dean Perkins offered the box of tissues to me and muttered his condolences. I swiped a few tissues and handed one to Mark. He dabbed at his eyes, and I did the same, catching more tears as they fell.

"We should go," Mark said, averting my gaze. "I have to plan your dad's funeral, and you need to pack your bags."

My uncle exchanged a few words with Dean Perkins, and then we exited his office, headed toward my new life with the Marshall boys.

Grace

I dropped the last pile of clothes onto my bed as my knees buckled beneath me. A blast of hot tears streamed down my cheeks, soaking the pale blue comforter. I cried out in physical pain, my heart broken and ripped to shreds.

None of this is real.

He's not dead.

This is a dream.

My body performed the motions as I packed my entire life into duffel bags. Two hours ago, I was eating lunch with Veronica, and now I was moving to Connecticut to live with my godfather and his sons.

"Sarge, get off the bed."

She rolled on top of my clothes, exposing her belly for me to rub.

"C'mon, girl, not now. We have to go. Uncle Mark is waiting for us."

She whimpered, and since I was a damn softie when it came to Sarge, I gave her a quick pat on her smooth stomach. Then, she stood on her short legs and jumped on me, paws digging into my chest.

"You're lucky," I whispered as she rubbed her wet nose on my neck. "You don't know he's gone yet."

Sarge licked my cheek.

My adorable English bulldog was the Marine Corps mascot. I fell in love with Sarge the second she jumped out of my dad's arms and licked my face. My dad had surprised me on my eighteenth birthday. He told me to think of Sarge as an extension of him.

"You're all I've got, girl." I kissed the top of her head. "Are you ready to live with Uncle Mark?"

She barked in response.

At least one of us was ready.

ON THE RIDE to Devil's Creek, Sarge fell asleep with her head on my lap. She snored as I stroked her silky coat with my fingers.

"Knox is allergic to dogs," Mark reminded me. "He's not going to be thrilled about having Sarge at the house. So, you'll have to keep her in your room."

Knox and Sloan were the youngest of the Marshall boys and fraternal twins. They were in their senior year of high school and had hit on me every summer since they figured out I had boobs. Cole was four years older than the boys and had noticed my growth spurt much sooner.

"Sarge is pretty low maintenance," I told Mark.

He nodded, his lips pressed into a thin line.

My dad used to say it was apparent Sarge was a Hale. So much like me, she could thrive in any situation. I had lived in cities around the world. Everywhere I went, I was the new girl. The outsider. It was nice to have Veronica for a few short months while I lived in Virginia Beach. For once, I felt normal, but I should have known it wouldn't last long.

Mark reached into his pocket and opened his palm to me. Silver dog tags shimmered against his tanned skin. Tears burned my eyes, but I didn't want to cry anymore. My head hurt from sobbing so hard.

I straightened my back against the leather seat and grabbed the tags, feeling the cold metal in my hand. "Is this all that's left of him?"

He turned his head to look out the window, unable to meet my gaze. "Close enough, I'm afraid."

I covered my mouth with my hand to mute the whimper that slipped from my lips. Sarge shifted her weight, moving her head to my thigh with a groan.

"It will be a closed casket."

Mark cleared his throat, though I could tell it was to stop himself from crying. We were both suppressing our emotions, pretending it didn't feel like we died along with him. Mark was like a brother to my dad. Neither of them had siblings. So, when they met at York Military Academy, they became brothers for life.

"I know this is hard for you, Grace, but we'll get through it together. If there's anything you need, just ask."

Mark came from old money, the kind of wealth that took decades to spend. Most of the men in his family had served in the military and then became politicians. His family created the Marshall Grant at York Military Academy that had allowed my dad to attend.

"I should be okay for a while. I don't need much."

Mark forced a closed-mouth smile.

I studied my dad's tags as we drove down the highway in the back of a stretch limousine, wondering what his last moments were like.

Did he think of me?

Was he afraid to die?

I wished I had the answers to those questions. But no one, not even Mark, could have known the answers. Mark still hadn't told me much about the accident. My dad was in a helicopter that caught fire during a training mission. He saved the passenger before the aircraft exploded.

Why couldn't he save himself? Why did he always have to be the hero? My dad was an action junkie who loved the thrill, a real-life superhero.

My very own Captain America.

After we exited the highway, we drove for close to

an hour before I could smell the bay. Mark lived in a seaside town called Devil's Creek, filled with billionaires and other rich pricks. They had more wealth than a small country with the political power and connections to match.

The people in Devil's Creek were unlike anyone I'd ever met. Men were power-hungry, and the women were so self-absorbed it was disgusting. It was like stepping into another world, one that didn't seem real enough to exist.

We drove through a neighborhood called The Hills, up a steep incline toward a guarded gate. The subdivision beyond the gate was known as Founders Way. A long stretch over the bay housed five mega-mansions that belonged to the founders of Devil's Creek.

As the tall iron gates opened for us, white lights illuminated the entrance to Fort Marshall, the last place on earth I wanted to live after Cole's hurtful text messages.

I should have run.

I wanted to run.

But I was out of options.

Out of cash and a place to live.

Fort Marshall had several guest houses, a pool house, and a massive garage with dozens of exotic cars. The driver parked in front of a three-story brick mansion that had at least a dozen windows with navy blue shutters.

A moment later, the driver opened the back door, welcoming us home. I'd never felt home any other place, and yet it was the last place I wanted to be. Sarge hopped off my lap and leaped out of the car to pee on the lawn. I tumbled out after her, and within seconds, she was at my side.

A short man with graying hair, dressed in a black suit with a red scarf tucked in the pocket, opened the front door. He lowered his head to Mark. "Welcome home, sir." He looked at me, a smile tugging at the corners of his mouth. "Welcome back, Miss Hale."

Mark nodded.

I smiled.

"Boys," Mark yelled as we stepped into the foyer.

No one answered.

He called out to his sons a few more times before three doors opened upstairs, and they staggered out of their bedrooms. The Marshall boys appeared in front of the railing that joined the twin staircases.

The younger boys had Mark's wavy black hair while Cole was blond like his mother. From the hard angles of their strong jaws to their perfectly chiseled cheekbones, they were beautiful. They all had the same blue eyes that reminded me of the ocean.

Knox shoved his hands into his jeans pockets. He

had short, dark curls tamed with gel, and Sloan kept his hair short. The twins were both gorgeous, but one look from Cole made my skin burn. It was as if he was touching me with his eyes, running his hands down my arms, leaving a trail of fire in his wake.

How could I hate him and still want him? It was ridiculous. I was an idiot for feeling anything for Cole after the way he treated me. His text message still filled my belly with dread.

Mark pointed his finger at the tiled floor in front of him and yelled, "Get down here. Now!"

Sloan rolled his eyes. Knox looked bored, staring down at the cell phone in his hand. Cole stood between his younger brothers, his face like a mask, not revealing a single thing. I could usually read between the lines with Cole. He never spoke much, but we never needed many words to communicate.

"Come say hello to Grace," Mark ordered.

Cole snorted, and his brothers cracked wicked smirks.

"Don't play games with me," Mark growled. "Not tonight. I'm not in the mood, boys."

The Marshall boys crossed their arms over their chests, glaring at me. I could have cared less if they didn't want me here because I didn't want to be here.

"Thank God we're going back to school after the funeral," Knox said under his breath. "I hate being in this fucking house with him."

"If you keep this shit up," Mark yelled, "you won't be going back to YMA. That would change all of your attitudes real quick."

"Don't even think about it," Cole challenged.

Knox rolled his shoulders as if he didn't have a care in the world. "And that would be on you if we fail out of school."

Cole leveled his father with one look and then aimed his hard, blue eyes at me.

"Hi, Grace," Sloan said with an attitude, then looked at his dad. "Happy?"

Sloan used to follow me around the house whenever I visited Fort Marshall. He'd once told me I was pretty and tried to play with my hair. Like I was his personal Barbie doll. Cole punched Sloan in the arm and told him to get lost, claiming me for himself.

The twins were sweet when they were kids, but Cole was never a good apple. He always toed the line between right and wrong. As I looked up at him, I could see he was the shell of the person I once knew. Cold and cruel, hardened by his mother's death.

Sarge barked at the boys. I ran my hand over the top of her head, proud of my baby for knowing a threat when she saw one.

I taught her well.

"That dog isn't staying in the house," Knox snapped.

"She'll live in Grace's bedroom," Mark told him. "I don't want to hear another word."

"This is bullshit," Knox said with so much hatred in his tone it burned my skin. "This is our house. Just because her dad died doesn't mean she gets a free pass to do whatever she wants."

"My brother is dead," Mark shouted, his voice wavering as he spoke. "I don't want to hear it, Knox. The dog stays. Deal with it."

"John wasn't your brother," Sloan retorted.

Mark's nostrils flared. "Sloan, Knox, carry John's footlocker upstairs for Grace." He tipped his head toward the open front door. "Cole, you can grab the rest of Grace's stuff."

Cole shot daggers at his dad. "Her hands don't look broken to me."

"We have staff for this pedestrian shit," Sloan chimed.

"Boys, don't start with me," Mark groaned. "If you want to keep your ranks at YMA, you will fall in line and do it fast."

Like their father, the boys were raised at York Military Academy and took their future military careers seriously. Mark's threat didn't go over well but did the job, forcing the boys to comply. They took their sweet ass time walking down the long staircase, glaring at me as they left the house.

A minute later, Knox and Sloan dropped my dad's

footlocker on the tiled floor in the middle of the foyer. Cole slung several duffel bags over his shoulders, his muscles flexing, and threw my clothes on top of the trunk.

"Upstairs," Mark snapped.

"She can sleep in the servant's quarters," Knox said with a bitter expression on his face. "With her dog." He covered his mouth and sneezed, turning his head away. "That fucking thing is going to be the death of me."

Mark pointed his finger at the stairs. "Upstairs, now! Grace is sleeping in your mother's old bedroom."

"No fucking way," Cole snapped. "She's not staying in Mom's room."

The twins echoed their sentiment with a few curses they muttered under their breaths.

When their mom was alive, the boys never messed with Mark. They treated him with respect. He wasn't just their father but also the Commandant of York Military Academy. On our ride to Fort Marshall, Mark had admitted that the boys blamed him for their mother's death. Because of their loss, they hated the world and everyone in it—including me.

"Let's go." Mark walked toward the stairs. "Drop the attitudes and get a move on." He extended his arm for me to go ahead of him. "I'll show you to your bedroom."

I cringed at the thought of sleeping in Willow's

room. When we were kids, I would sit with Cole and watch her play the piano. She was a concert pianist and a damn good one. Willow always had a smile on her face and a song on her lips. She was eccentric and funny, the mother I had always wanted.

I still couldn't comprehend the events surrounding her death. Cole found her body floating at the top of the pool, her wrists sliced and drained of blood. No one knew what happened. The police called it a suicide. All of the signs pointed to that. Except she didn't leave a note. She never showed a single sign she was depressed.

Knox and Sloan set my dad's footlocker in front of the bed in Willow's old room. Sloan let out an obnoxious groan as if carrying the chest drained all of his energy. They stared around the vast room that had high ceilings, a large four-poster bed at the center, and a grand piano by the wall of windows, which overlooked the bay. It was soundproof, so Willow could compose into the wee hours of the morning, losing herself to the muse.

A few years ago, I'd heard Cole slip out of his bedroom in the middle of the night. I was staying with his family for the summer and couldn't sleep. So, I crept down the hall and found him lowering a blanket over his mother.

She'd fallen asleep on the bench in front of the piano with her fingers still on the keys. He watched over her as she slept. And I watched him because I loved how his stony demeanor always softened around his mom. She was the only person, other than me, who could reach him.

Now he was lost.

Cole threw my bags in front of the walk-in closet. "Don't touch any of her stuff." He gave his father a disgusted look. "She shouldn't be in here."

"The arrangement is only temporary," Mark said. "Stop acting like a spoiled brat."

Sloan shook his head at his dad. "We have fifteen bedrooms, and you have to give her Mom's?"

Knox glared at his dad and shoved his hands into his pockets.

Mark pressed his thumbs to his eyes and groaned. "Get out. Just get the hell out of here. I don't want to see any of you until dinner."

"We don't want to eat dinner with you or your charity case," Cole said with disdain. "You can count us out."

Cole left the bedroom, followed by Sloan, then Knox, who slammed the door behind him.

"I'm sorry about that," Mark said with a sigh. "They've been like this since Willow." He pinched the bridge of his nose between his fingers. "I don't know what to do anymore. First Willow, and now John."

"I can handle them. I've dealt with much worse than a few spoiled boys."

His blue eyes were glassy when they met mine. "I'll let you get settled. Dinner is in one hour in the main dining room."

Mark left me alone, surrounded by everything that reminded me of Willow and what her family lost.

Grace

I cracked open my bedroom door and poked my head into the hallway. After the boys had stormed out of the room, rap music blared throughout the house. Mark shouted threats until the music ceased.

Since then, I hadn't heard a sound. I closed the door and glanced over the railing, checking for the Marshall boys. Relief washed over me, and for a moment, I wondered if they had left the house for the night.

I took the staircase to my left and headed toward the kitchen. My nose tipped up at the scent of beef and steamed vegetables. The smell triggered memories of the past, taking me back to the last night I spent with my dad.

I found Mark in the main dining room. He sat at the head of the table by himself, drinking a glass of scotch as he read the newspaper in his other hand. The complete opposite of my dad, he reminded me of a businessman, not a military academy's commandant.

"Did I miss dinner?" I asked Mark from the dining room entrance.

He looked up from the newspaper. "No, you're right on schedule."

I sat in the chair beside him. "Is it just the two of us?"

Mark folded the paper in half and set it on the table beside him. "For now."

"Did the boys leave?"

He shook his head. "They're around here somewhere, probably waiting to stir up more trouble."

"I didn't mean to start problems for you by coming here."

"This isn't about you, Grace. The boys haven't been the same since Willow's death, Cole most of all." His eyes drifted to the table, and he blew out a deep breath. "He found his mother floating in a pool of blood. That's not something any child should ever see."

I cupped my knees with my hands to steady my trembling fingers. "I tried talking to Cole after Willow passed. He pushed me away. So did Hunter."

"He'll come around," he said, though his voice lacked confidence. "One day, Cole will come to terms with his pain. He hasn't begun healing. Hunter is just doing what Cole wants because he thinks it's the right thing to do. I wouldn't take it personally."

"I'm trying, but I could use my friends right now."

"I'm sorry, Grace."

"Knox and Sloan seem like they're holding it in, too," I said to change the subject from me.

I hated being the center of attention.

Mark bobbed his head in agreement. "We're all doing the best we can to keep it together. It hasn't been easy without Willow around. She was like a ray of sunshine that lit up our world."

My heart ached at his sweet words. He loved his wife. Anyone who saw them together could read it on his face, see it in the way he treated her.

"Willow was an incredible woman," I said and meant it. "She was the mother I always wanted."

"She looked forward to your summer visits. Willow wanted a daughter, but we had all boys. She thought of you as her daughter."

I smiled, a real one that reached my eyes. "It would have been nice to have a mom, especially during my awkward teenage years."

Mark tipped back his drink, and his shoulders slumped against the chair as if he were at ease for the first time in a long time. A server set our plates on the table in front of us, then exited the room through a door on the left which led to the Butler's kitchen.

I sliced into my steak and almost cried at the thought of my dad and our last meal together. I kept replaying our last moments, attempting to memorize every second, so I could remember them forever. I wondered if Mark was doing the same thing.

Did he roam around this monstrous house and catalog every detail of his life with Willow until her tragic end? I never cared much about moving around with my dad. But now, I wished we'd had a home.

Tears stung my eyes, and I blinked them away. Mark watched me with concern scrolling across his face. He looked as if he'd aged ten years since the summer.

"I was planning to stay in Virginia Beach with my dad after his retirement. But that's not an option anymore. It's too expensive to live there on my own."

"If you need money," Mark said between bites of steak, "I can help you out, Grace. I have more money at my disposal than I can spend in my lifetime."

I smiled at his offer. "Thank you, Uncle Mark. I appreciate it. But I can't take your money."

"So much like your dad." He leaned back in the high-back wooden chair and rested his elbow on the arm. "He refused me every time."

"He lived a simple life. My dad didn't grow up with money."

"That's why I've kept his funeral simple. Just some old friends and co-workers."

"This still doesn't feel real."

Mark rubbed at the corner of his eye and turned his head. "You always have a home here, Grace."

Before I could respond, Cole stumbled into the dining room with a bottle of Jack Daniels raised to his mouth. He didn't even look in my direction. Mark glared at his son, teeth gritted as Cole drank from the bottle.

"I need to talk to you," Cole mumbled. "Alone."

"We're in the middle of dinner." Mark extended his hand to the empty chair beside him. "Sit and eat with us. We can talk afterward."

"No." Cole clenched his jaw, his grip tightening on the bottle. "We need to talk. Now. It's about the Knights."

The Knights?

Mark shot a glance at me, then dropped his fork onto his plate. "Excuse us," he said to me, then led a drunken Cole out of the dining room.

MARK LEFT in the middle of dinner and never returned. I waited for over an hour, taking my time eating dessert and drinking coffee without a single sign of the Marshalls. I didn't know if they were still in the house or had gone somewhere to deal with Cole's issue with the Knights. Whatever that meant. I'd never heard Cole or Mark mention the Knights before.

I spent the rest of the night in my bedroom re-reading the first Harry Potter book. Whenever in doubt, I always turned to one of my comfort reads to take my mind off things. I read half the book before I heard a disturbance in the hallway. It sounded like something slammed into the wall, followed by a thud.

What the hell?

I glanced over at the clock, surprised it was well after two o'clock in the morning. Time had escaped me. When I'd started reading, it was a little after nine.

I kept telling myself one more chapter and then bed. But the book just kept getting better and better, too good for me to put down. I both loved and hated when that happened. Sleep was great, but so was getting lost in a good book.

Another loud noise made my heart race, and the hairs on my arms stood at attention. Sarge awoke from her slumber on the bed beside me. Her eyes darted around the room, searching for the source.

"It's okay, girl. Go back to sleep."

I stuffed the bookmark into the fold of the book and set it on the nightstand. Footsteps sounded on the hardwood in the hallway, coming closer to my bedroom. I shot up from the bed, raced across the room, and flipped the lock on the door. Sarge was by my side and jumped up on the wood. The footsteps stopped right in front of me.

I heard someone breathing on the other side, but maybe it was my imagination. Nerves coursed through my body, causing my hands and legs to tremble. Someone turned the doorknob, which spun but refused to open.

Sarge barked at the intruder.

I wondered if it was Cole coming to make amends. Or if it was a drunken Cole, who was looking for a quick fuck after a long night of drinking. It didn't matter. There was no way I would talk to him when he wasn't in his right mind.

I lifted Sarge into my arms, scratching behind her ears until shoes tapped on the floor, moving away from my room. The tension in my body slowly faded, and a few minutes passed without another sound. So I slid onto the mattress with Sarge, grabbed the book, and laid my head on the pillow. Sarge resumed her position beside me, closing her eyes with her chin on my thigh.

I flipped the book open to the last page I'd read and tried to relax. With the funeral in the morning, I doubted I would get any sleep. My body was in over-drive from all the adrenaline pumping through my veins. I wanted to focus on anything other than my dad. Until the funeral, I could pretend this was all a dream.

After a while, I fell into a steady groove. My eyes fluttered with each page I turned, and I no longer had the energy to focus on the words. They blurred together into a mess of lines. My eyes closed for a second before I heard metal grinding.

What the fuck?

Propping myself up on my elbow, I looked for the source, but before I could react, my bedroom door flung open. Cole stood in the entryway, dressed in jeans and a fitted black shirt that clung to his muscles like armor. Even drunk, with one eye slightly closed, he still looked like a god, oozing sex appeal.

"What are you doing in here?" I demanded. "I'm sleeping."

Sarge leaped forward as he entered the room, and I had to grab her collar before she attacked him.

He dangled a key from a long string and approached the bed with caution. "You can't stay here, Grace."

"In your mom's room? Yes, I know it bothers you."

"It's not just her room." He stopped at the edge of the bed and glared at me. "You can't stay in Devil's Creek. After the funeral, you need to leave."

"Why do you hate me so much? Tell me why you stopped talking to me, why you shut me out. Because I don't get it."

Cole pressed his palms to the mattress, a scary expression aimed at me. He looked like he wasn't sure if he wanted to fuck me or kill me. I was hoping for neither option at this point. He was too much of a bastard for me to let him crawl between my legs again.

"You being here will ruin everything," he said, his top lip quivering in anger. "Leave before I make you."

"What's with all the games, Cole? Tell me the truth. Explain why you think I should leave."

He leaned forward, his hand balled into a fist on

the mattress, those beautiful blue eyes fixed on me. "Trust me, Grace. A lot of shit has gone down since you moved to Virginia. If I had it my way, I would send you halfway around the world."

"Why are you trying so hard to get rid of me?"

He leveled me with an evil stare. "There are things you don't understand about my world. Things you couldn't even comprehend."

I crossed my arms under my breasts, attempting to hide my nipples that poked through the silky pajama top. "What are you talking about, Cole?"

He shook his head, and the scent of hard liquor rolled off him. "Just go, Grace. If you ever gave a damn about me, listen to what I'm telling you."

Without another word, he stormed out of the room and slammed the door behind him.

Cole

I paced down the hallway outside of Grace's bedroom. My mother's old bedroom. I couldn't stand the thought of anyone inside that room other than my mom.

It was stupid and petty.

Grace had just lost her dad, and my mom wouldn't have cared if she were still alive, but I wasn't ready to disrupt the shrine we had resurrected in her honor. We hadn't touched a single thing in that room, taking turns visiting it like a museum.

She had to leave town before I forced her. The Knights were in danger, which meant everyone in our lives was at risk. Just being associated with us was deadly.

First my mother.

Then John Hale.

The Colonel wasn't a Knight and never could have been because of his upbringing, but he was working with us before his death. And his help had gotten him killed.

"Cole," my dad warned.

I cocked my head toward the stairs. He waited for me with his hand on the railing. In a matter of months, he looked as if he'd aged years from carrying the weight of our world on his shoulders.

All of us were feeling the pain.

The house had grown silent and violent, none of us able to communicate our feelings. We hadn't been able to talk to each other since my mom's death. Every conversation turned into an argument.

"Leave her alone," Dad ordered.

"Don't tell me what to do. Grace is leaving Devil's Creek after the funeral."

He approached me with caution, his eyes fiery and intense. "Grace is my responsibility now. And I say she stays."

"You can't fix everyone. This isn't your problem to solve."

"We talked about this, Cole. Grace will be safe at the academy. The matter isn't up for debate." He slapped his hand on my back, pushing me down the corridor. "Go back to sleep. John's funeral is in four hours."

"As if I can sleep with all the shit we're dealing with."

"You don't have to be a Knight at all times." He tipped his head toward my bedroom. "Now, go. You need to rest." His nose wrinkled in disgust as he leaned closer. "No more binge drinking. I don't want Grace to see you like this."

"Like what, Dad?"

"Cole, this isn't like you. I raised you to be a better man. Act like it."

I folded my arms over my chest and breathed through my nose to quell my anger. "I'm trying to be a better man. But you won't let me."

"Stop making everything about Grace. We can protect her at the academy."

"The cadets will eat her alive. You're throwing her to the wolves."

"Then, you better protect her from threats."

I shook my head. "No, I'll make sure she leaves and never comes back. I will make every day at that school feel like her worst nightmare. And by the time I'm done with her, she'll wish she had listened to me."

He pursed his lips. "Don't interfere with The Founders Society. It will not end well for you."

"I don't care about the Founders. Grace is mine. I won't let them have her."

"Cole, you know how important she is to the cause. My ass is on the line, too. The Lucaya Group is closer than ever. It's only a matter of time before they find Grace. Don't fuck this up for us."

Ignoring his request, I stormed down the hall toward my bedroom. Once inside, I leaned my back against the wall and blew out a deep breath. Because of my father's insistence to follow the Founders' rules, I had to do the worst thing imaginable to Grace—make her hate me so much she would never speak to me again.

But it was for her own good.

Grace

Tears spilled down my cheeks as I stared at my father's casket. Before my dad left for his mission, I begged him not to go. I had a bad feeling, one I could not shake.

My dad had cupped my cheek and said, "Gracie, I named you after the first female admiral for a reason. You're strong. You're a fighter. You can do anything when you set your mind to it." He swiped my tears away with his thumb, his jaw hard as stone when he looked into my eyes. "I'll be home before you know it. I promise."

My heart ached from the loss, the pain so intense my entire body was numb. I felt like I was dying, so hollow, empty, and alone. Like I wanted to climb into the coffin with him.

Well over a hundred people gathered around me, but I could count on one hand how many of them I knew. Hunter was here with his family. His brothers looked just like him, tall and with the same dark hair and green eyes. A few times, I caught him staring at me, wishing he would stop acting like a jerk and comfort me.

Mark stood at my side, towering over me as he placed a gloved hand on my shoulder for support. Most of the men and women in the crowd wore the Marine Corps dress blue uniform, the same one my father wore on special occasions.

When I was a kid, I would sit on my dad's bed and watch him iron his uniforms. And as the years ticked by, he showed me how to do it myself. Those moments were so simple, routine. The hole in my chest cracked open, pain spreading throughout my trembling body.

I clutched Mark's hand.

"It's okay, Gracie," he said low enough not to disrupt the chaplain.

After I stopped crying, Mark released his grip on me. I hated wearing heels. My feet were killing me, making the ceremony even more unbearable. The soft dirt beneath my feet wedged my shoe deeper into the grass, holding me in place.

I stared at my father's casket, still in disbelief he was inside. How could we amass so much in life and leave this world in a stupid box? I didn't know what came over me, but I had the sudden urge to touch his casket. I wasn't ready to lose my father for good.

Was anyone, though?

I stepped forward, but with my heel stuck in the damn patch of grass, I fell forward. My fingers gripped the edge of the American flag that slid across the wood. And now, I had disgraced him.

Shit. Pull yourself together, Grace.

Mark fixed the flag before anyone noticed. Well, almost anyone. His sons were a few paces to his left, all three of them staring at me with a mixture of pity and irritation.

The Marshall boys hated me.

They didn't want me in their lives.

I was their father's latest charity case.

After the funeral ended, a Marine with cropped reddish-brown hair, tanned skin, and kind eyes approached me. A dimple creased his left cheek as he gave me the cutest smile. My expression mirrored his, quickly entranced by the gorgeous Marine. He was in his mid-twenties and looked like he could grace the cover of *GQ*, the sexy Marines edition.

"Grace." He extended his hand to me. "I'm sorry about your dad." I nodded, and he continued, "Colonel Hale was a good Marine." As I shook his hand, he said, "I'm Oliver."

Even his name was cute.

"I owe your father a debt I can never repay. If you ever need anything…"

"I need answers."

He gripped my bicep and pulled me beneath a tree. Lowering his voice, he glanced over his shoulder and whispered, "The people closest to you are lying. If you want answers about your dad, go to York Military Academy."

Before I could respond, Mark called out my name. Oliver tensed at the sound of his voice, then let his hand fall from my arm, taking a few steps back. Was he afraid of Mark?

"Commandant," Oliver said to my uncle.

Then he walked away, looking over his shoulder at me one last time before he rejoined his friends. Why did he owe my dad a favor? And why did he want me to go to the academy?

Mark touched my shoulder. "Time to go, Grace."

On the ride home, you could cut the tension with a knife. The awkward silence in the limo was almost unbearable. Knox and Sloan sat across from me with Cole and Mark on my left. Cole lounged by the window with his ankles crossed. His black dress shoes were so shiny I could use them as a mirror.

The Marshalls' uniforms reminded me of my dad and the one he would never wear again. We would never get to dance together at the Marine Corps Ball. It was the one night every year when we'd dress up and stuff our faces. I missed him so much it felt like my chest cracked open and my insides spilled onto the floor.

My dad would want me to be strong.

I am strong.

I can do this.

When we were kids, Cole would pull my pigtails and chase me around the mansion. He was my best friend, my everything. I wanted so badly to throw myself into his arms. Desperate for his warmth, I would have done anything for a second alone with the boy I once loved. The boy who I thought, at one time, might have loved me back.

Apart from Grams, who was also dead, I didn't have any other family. I was never close to cousins or aunts, moving too often to know anyone. The Marshalls were the one constant in my life, the only family I needed.

Now, they were all I had left.

"Grace." Mark's voice cut through the silence. "I was going to tell you this over dinner, but it can't wait. Starting tomorrow, you're our newest recruit at York Military Academy. Our first female cadet."

The twins gasped in unison.

My mouth dropped in shock. "Cadet?"

"You mean plebe," Sloan interjected. "No one walks into YMA and becomes a cadet on the first day."

Mark nodded. "Yes, that's true. I'm not bending the rules for Grace, so don't worry. Just like you and your brothers, Grace will become a cadet after she completes cadet training."

"But I'm a girl," I pointed out.

I considered Oliver's words for a moment. He was trying to warn me that the people closest to me were lying. Based on his reaction to my uncle, I assumed he meant the Marshalls. I wanted answers about my dad, and if they were at York Military Academy, then that was where I would go.

Cole leaned forward, his blue eyes intense. "If you even think about stepping foot on campus, you'll regret it."

His warning sent a shiver down my arms.

"Don't listen to the boys," Mark said. "A Marine raised you. You'll be a natural at the academy."

"We'll see about that," Cole muttered.

I glanced at the epaulettes on Cole's shoulders, noting his insignia, which indicated he was a cadet colonel at York Military Academy. Of course, he was an officer, which meant my life was about to get much more complicated.

Grace

York Military Academy was an impenetrable fortress on the coast of Connecticut. From the window of the stretch limousine, I could see the guard gate in the distance. Heard the sound of waves crashing below us, a reminder I had no escape from this place.

The closest town was over thirty miles away. A thought that stirred my belly with nerves, making it impossible for me to sit still without fidgeting. This was my new home for the foreseeable future if I wanted answers about my dad's death. I had to follow through with the plan and become the first female cadet.

Sarge sat on the bench beside me, curled up against my thigh. She fell asleep ten minutes into our ride. Mark said she could live with him on campus at the commandant's house, where I could visit her on weekends.

When we stopped at the gate, Mark rolled down the back window and greeted the guard. He wore navy blue fatigues and a matching garrison cap, which had a gold YMA logo emblazoned on the fabric. The

Marshalls wore their uniforms, looking like muscled military perfection. I was the only one who stood out from the group dressed in civilian clothes.

Mark chatted with the guard for a minute, and then he waved us through the gate. I pressed my face to the window and noted the Gothic architecture that seemed out of place at a military school. York Military Academy was unlike other institutions. Classes ranged from middle school to college, all under one command, with grade levels separated by company.

We headed down a pathway to our right, where a big sign for the college read Alpha Company. Bravo Company, the high school, was to our left, and if you followed the path around the perimeter of the compound, you'd find Charlie Company, the middle school. Uncle Mark was the commandant and had the entire command under his authority.

Mark tapped me on the shoulder. "We'll drop you and Cole off first."

"Sounds good."

"My assistant left your uniforms, welcome packet, and supplies in your living quarters. If you need anything, just let me know." My uncle lifted his arm and glanced at his watch. "I have to stop at the office first, but I can come back to your barracks and give you a tour."

"No," Cole interrupted. "I'll show her around."

Mark's nose scrunched. "No funny business."

Cole snorted with laughter.

"I mean it, Cole."

Cole rolled his eyes, leaning back against the leather bench with his arms folded over his thick chest.

"I'll be fine," I assured Mark. "I don't want or need you to give me preferential treatment. It will only make things worse."

"She already has a target on her back," Knox chimed.

"Bullseye," Sloan said with laughter in his tone, pointing his finger at my head like he was shooting a gun.

"Yeah, I get it," I fired back. "None of you want me here. Fine with me. I can handle myself."

"This won't be an easy transition, Grace." Mark sighed. "I've had a lot of complaints from donors and parents about you attending the academy. The cadets won't welcome you with open arms. But I have faith that you'll win them over."

"She can't spread her legs for every guy at school," Sloan joked.

"Or maybe she can," Knox muttered to his twin, laughing.

"She's hot but not *that* hot," Sloan whispered with his head down, leaning into his brother.

"No one at this school is touching her," Cole cut in. "So shut the fuck up."

I almost wanted to thank him for sticking up for

me. Was he finally coming around? Would Cole be an ally at this school? Only one way to find out.

"I expect you to watch out for Grace," Mark said to Cole.

"I already told you how this would play out, *Commandant.*"

"Don't you dare screw with me, boy."

Cole slid across the bench and got in Mark's face. "You won't be around every minute of the day to protect your precious cargo. And I'm not a boy, so stop treating me like one."

"If you do anything stupid," Mark said in a threatening tone, "I will have you court-martialed and thrown in the brig for the rest of the semester."

As we parked in front of our dormitory, Mark said to me, "Don't underestimate the challenges you will face. For the first eight weeks, you'll go through cadet training. Only thirty percent of our recruits make it beyond the first few weeks."

"I've been preparing for this my entire life. My dad made sure I could handle anything."

Mark grinned. "That's why I think you'll be the perfect test case."

"For what?"

"To show the board women can handle the rigorous training."

"I'll become a cadet," I said with certainty.

"Not if I have anything to do with it," Cole

snapped. "You don't belong here, Grace. I told you to leave. You didn't listen. Just remember I warned you."

A wave of anger heated my skin as I turned to face Cole. "Don't threaten me. You, of all people, know what I'm capable of."

Mark leaned over and opened the door, his gaze aimed at me. "Knox and Sloan are in Bravo Company." He pointed out the door to our left. "My office is in Harper Hall, at the back of the academy. If anyone bothers you, or you run into trouble, come get me."

"She's not a snitch," Cole told him, then climbed out of the car without saying goodbye to his family.

Mark shook his head. "Ignore Cole. You can do this, Grace. Don't let them see you sweat."

"I never do," I said before I hopped out of the limo.

Sarge jumped up on my thighs. I bent down to pet her head and gave her a few kisses. "I'll come see you soon. Be good for Uncle Mark." I set her down on the floor near Mark's shiny dress shoe. "Thank you," I said to him before Cole slammed the door.

He dragged me across the flagstones like a child, tugging my wrist so hard my skin burned. "Alpha Company spans the south side of the campus." Cole waved his hand at the four buildings interspersed along the Quad. "You'll attend classes in these buildings if you last until your first day."

I shook him off me. "Cole, why are you acting like such an asshole?"

"Because it's the only way."

"We have known each other for most of our lives. You've never treated me like this. What the fuck is wrong with you?"

He rolled his shoulders, nonchalant. "Where would I even begin?"

"If you want to point me toward the barracks, I can find my way around."

I stopped at the center of the path, looking out of place in street clothes. My skinny jeans clung to my thighs like plastic wrap, and the thin baby tee just barely covered my stomach. Cole stood so close I could feel his breath on my forehead.

I was afraid to look up at him. Because I knew if I did, I would allow my feelings for him to make excuses for why he had turned into a monster. I wanted to believe my best friend was still inside that gorgeous body, though it was his mind that concerned me. He was not himself, despite still looking the same as he had over the summer.

"Cole," I whispered. "Please stop torturing me and tell me what's wrong."

"You should be more concerned about what the cadets will do when they see you. Don't worry about me. I'm no longer your concern."

"I hate you," I shot back, even though I didn't mean it.

"Good." He smirked. "It will make this a lot easier for both of us if you do."

I followed Cole to Bryant Hall, which was to our right. Dozens of students assembled in the courtyard between the buildings, lounging on the benches. Heads snapped in our direction. And as we approached my new living quarters, all eyes were on me.

Some guys tipped their heads at Cole in greeting. Undeterred, he held his head high and kept his gaze on our final destination. I spotted Hunter on our way toward the double doors.

"Hey," I said to Hunter, whose face illuminated as his eyes traveled up and down my body. He towered over me, his muscles bulging from beneath his blazer.

Hunter glanced at Cole as if he needed his permission to speak to me. Cole shook his head, communicating a silent message to Hunter.

I slammed my palm into Hunter's chest and muttered, "What is it with you two? Why don't you just fuck already?"

As I walked away, Hunter grabbed my bicep and pulled me into his muscular chest. "Watch it, Hale."

Disappointed with his attitude, I shook my head. "And here I thought we could still be friends. Guess I was wrong about both of you."

Hunter pressed his lips against the shell of my ear,

making my skin tingle. "Kinda hard to be friends with someone when you know the sounds they make when they come."

For a moment, I got swept up in the feeling of his strong hands on my body and his delicious, manly scent. Then I came to my senses. He was no longer my friend, and I shouldn't even bother trying to force him to like me anymore.

It wasn't worth my time.

"If that's true," I said, "then how are you and Cole still friends?"

He pretended he didn't hear me and looked at Cole. "We moved her to the officer's quarters."

Cole tugged on my arm for me to follow him into the building. "You're gonna love your new room," he said with a creepy grin stretched across his full lips.

"Which means I'll probably hate it."

As Cole walked into the building, the cadets parted for their king. At this school, people treated him like royalty. He'd spent his entire life on this campus and was the heir apparent to replace his father.

Cole walked through the building, stepping into his role as my tour guide. "All of the college students are in Alpha Company, which is split into four platoons, one for each year. You'll be with Hunter and me in First Platoon. Our quarters are on the top deck. Second Platoon is on the first deck. Third Platoon and Fourth

Platoon are in Weaver Hall, the building on the other side of the courtyard."

We took the stairs at the end of the long hallway, and Cole continued his spiel. "You're not to associate with the cadets in the other platoons. So don't bother trying to make friends with any of them."

"Each year, we compete for the Command Cup," Hunter interjected. "We record our academic and athletic achievements, and at the end of the year, we total the number and compete against each other in the War Games to see who takes home the trophy."

"So it's like winning the Hogwarts House Cup. Let me guess. We're in Slytherin."

Hunter laughed. "Not quite, sweetheart."

Pushing his way through the crowd, Cole led the way. "I'm the platoon commander," he said with authority. "Hunter is the platoon sergeant. You answer to us and no one else. And don't get fucking cute with me."

I looked up at Hunter, who grinned like a psychopath.

"They must be desperate to put the two of you in charge of a platoon."

"You'll go through cadet training with freshman and incoming upperclassmen," Cole added.

"Watch me dance circles around them."

Cole grabbed my shoulder and shoved me into the wall. He invaded my senses, leaning down to speak against my lips. "Let's get something straight, *Hale*. You're not one of us. You will never be one of us."

"I'm not afraid of you."

His lips were inches from mine, his breath heating my skin. He moved his hands to the wall on each side of my head. I tried to steady my breathing and failed miserably. He smelled too good, his warm, hard body pressed against mine. Cole's pretty blue eyes bore into mine as if he were staring into the depths of my soul.

"Cole," I whispered.

As if his name snapped him back to reality, he pushed off from the wall, stepped back, and cleared his throat. Five guys walked past us in their uniforms and tipped their heads to Cole and Hunter. Their gazes traveled up and down the length of my skin-tight jeans and to the swell of my breasts.

The tallest of the group licked his lips when his eyes met mine. A dark-haired man with tattoos on his right forearm raised his arm and slid his finger across his neck. My eyes met the blond-haired hottie on his left, who looked like a model dressed for a military photo shoot. The other two guys were dark-haired, filled out in the chest and arms.

A shiver rushed down my arms. Panic shot through my chest, and for the first time since I stepped onto the grounds, I considered Cole's threat. I was in danger here. Maybe I shouldn't have come to this damn school.

When he invited himself into my bedroom and warned me to leave, I thought little of it. Cole would never hurt me. At least I never thought he would, not until he ghosted me and turned into an entirely different person. He was never a monster. I kept telling myself that as I stared into his eyes, noting the darkness that had fallen over his handsome features.

He wasn't *my* Cole anymore.

As I watched the guys disappear down the hallway, I swallowed the lump forming at the back of my throat. They would join Cole in his attempt to get rid of me. No one wanted me here, but I only needed one ally, someone with enough power to neutralize the threat.

"It's not too late to leave," Cole said in a taunting tone, a smirk tugging at his gorgeous mouth. "The gates are still open."

"No one will think less of you." Hunter shoved a hand through his short, dark hair, his expression hard. "You don't belong here, Grace. I don't want to see you get hurt."

I moved my hands to my hips, pushing out my chest. "Why are the two of you trying so hard to get rid of me?"

Cole's eyes fell to my cleavage. Hunter's gaze also wandered for a moment, then went right back to my face.

"This isn't about me being the only girl at the academy."

"It has everything to do with that," Cole fired back.

"You're disrupting the natural order," Hunter said. "Most of the plebes can't make it past the first few weeks of training. Everyone on campus will see to it that you fail. They don't want the board to approve women at YMA. So you have to fail. They won't stop until you do."

I tucked my trembling lip into my mouth to steady my nerves. With my arms crossed, I squared off with my cadets. "You're looking at the first female cadet. I won't let a bunch of bullies deter me from my goal."

A satisfied grin crept across Hunter's face. He was trying so hard to be on Cole's side, but I could tell he still cared about me. Unfortunately, I wouldn't get his help publicly. So I had to get him away from Cole. They couldn't spend every moment of the day together. There had to be a gap in their schedules that would allow me to isolate Hunter without Cole breathing down our backs.

Cole opened the last door at the end of the hallway, and my mouth dropped in horror. They trashed the single-occupant room, throwing the sheets on the floor, the furniture turned over. There wasn't a single thing that wasn't broken, tipped on its side, or ripped to shreds.

"Better get cleaning." Hunter roared with laughter.

"You don't want to fail inspection. It's a strike against our platoon."

"We'll lose points?"

He nodded.

"Only officers have private rooms," Cole said, with a hint of anger in his tone. "You would normally sleep in a shared room with cadets of equal rank. But since you're a woman, the commandant has given you the staff officer's quarters."

I looked at Cole before inching my way into the messy room. "I told your dad I didn't want special treatment."

"You won't last a week," Cole quipped with way too much enthusiasm. "There's one more thing the guys wanted me to tell you." He bent down, his breath on my cheek. "Compliments of First Platoon."

Hunter laughed before closing the door behind them.

Grace

I stood at the center of the destroyed room. Cole wasn't joking when he said he wanted me gone. That I should run while the gates were still open. If this was what I could expect from First Platoon, I would have to fight like hell to survive.

The cadets busted my bed, the wood fractured in several places. A few hours after I started cleaning my room, it still looked like a bomb had detonated. Cole and his cadet friends had given a new meaning to fuck my life. The floors and walls were covered in grime.

I needed paint and better cleaning supplies to whip this place back into shape. Without tools, I couldn't fix this mess. I could have told my uncle Mark what the boys did to my living quarters. But that would have made me more of an outcast.

I had to show the cadets that ruined uniforms and broken furniture wouldn't break my spirit. So I got to work and lifted the twin mattress and lowered it onto the cracked frame. Once I had the mattress in place, I grabbed the dirty sheets from the floor. My stomach clenched as I gripped the fabric in my hands, thinking about one of my dad's many lessons.

Dad crossed his arms over his chest, inspecting my failed attempt at making the bed properly. "Square corners, Gracie."

I sighed as I stared down at the bed I'd just made. No matter how tight I pulled the sheets, I could never get it right. "But I made the bed."

"Do you know why you have to make your bed every day?"

I glanced up at him. "Because you make me."

"Yes, but do you know why it's important to start your day with a simple task like making your bed?"

I shook my head. "It's just a bed, Daddy. Why does it matter if the sheets are perfect?"

"It's not about the sheets, Grace. I'm trying to instill the importance of starting every morning with a simple task. Making your bed gives you a sense of accomplishment before your day begins. And if you can do this one small task, it will be easier for you to complete another and then another. Good habits are important. They build character and help you achieve success." A beat passed between us before he added, "Now strip off the sheets and start over."

"Yes, sir."

He patted me on the back and smiled. "That's my girl."

I never complained. Dad constantly reminded me that complaints caused problems and never offered solutions. My dad was the reason I was so disciplined and could get through anything. No task was ever too hard for him. And because of him, I could survive one year at York Military Academy.

As I wiped down the furniture, someone knocked on the door, snapping me back to reality. I stood painfully still with a wet rag in my hand. It was one of the few usable things left in the bathroom. My platoon had dragged every single towel and washcloth through the mud. The boys even went as far as painting the bathroom walls with the same filth.

"Grace," Hunter boomed in that deep voice that rolled over my skin. "Let me in."

I dropped the rag onto the table and swung open the door. My mouth fell open at the sight of Hunter in all of his glory. He looked like a muscled military god, his broad shoulders and huge biceps even more prominent beneath the navy blue academy blazer.

"You look like shit," he said as he appraised my appearance. "What the fuck happened to you?"

I frowned at his comment. "Thanks a lot, Hunter. And for the record, you and your friends happened to me."

"Take a shower." He stepped forward, pushing his way inside. "It's almost time for the swearing-in ceremony."

"When is it?"

"At 1400 hours." He closed the door. "In Marshall Hall."

Of course, there was a building on campus named

after the King of the Dicks. Cole had told me stories about his time at the academy, and around here, people followed Marshall Law.

No one would ever defy him.

If he wanted me gone, the cadets would find a way, so I needed an ally.

I licked my lips, drinking in Hunter's manly scent, trying not to focus on how good he looked in his uniform—not thinking about those hard muscles flexing beneath the navy blazer that molded to his biceps. "Will you be there?"

He nodded. "All hands."

"Thanks to First Platoon, I have nothing to wear." I pointed at the torn and dirty uniforms on the floor beside the chest of drawers.

His eyes followed where my finger landed. The slightest frown tugged at his lips.

"I know you weren't part of this, Hunter." I gripped his tie in my hand and stood on my tippy toes. He was so damn tall it was like trying to climb a tree to reach his lips. "You wouldn't do this to me."

He sighed. "I'm sorry, Grace. The Marshalls run this school."

I slipped my fingers through his hair and pulled his lips to mine. "Please, Hunter. I'm out of my element here. I'm in the middle of nowhere Connecticut with no money, friends, or a connection to the real world.

Once upon a time, you and Cole were my friends. We had each other's backs."

"Grace, I can't."

I traced my fingers down his muscular chest and stopped at the waistband of his trousers. His breathing labored, chest rising and falling as my fingers slipped beneath his pants.

"Fuck," he whispered as I inched lower. "C'mon, Grace."

"Please, Hunter." I brushed my lips against his, then shoved my hand into his boxers. "Help me out, and I'll take good care of you. I'm the only woman at this school. I can make the next year good for you if you return the favor."

I'd never had a problem getting him to do what I wanted. The second I touched Hunter, I had him. He stumbled backward into the door, and I unbuttoned his pants, pulling out his cock. Eyes closed, he breathed out his nose and rested his head against the door. His cock was long and thick and so big in my small hand.

"Did you miss this, Hunter?" I whispered the words against his mouth, then sucked on his bottom lip. "Huh? Tell me how much you missed me."

His eyes shot open, then his hand flew to the back of my head, fingers slipping through my hair. "Yeah, baby girl. I missed you."

"I won't tell Cole." I worked him into a frenzy, and

his eyes widened. "This will be our secret. But you better not fuck me over."

"I won't," he muttered as he raced toward the finish line. "Fuck, baby, I'm so close."

I released a moan as I jerked his shaft, which only made him breathe deeper, bending down to grunt in my ear. He sucked my earlobe into his mouth, his skilled tongue driving me wild. His big hands roamed over my shoulders, then traced the tops of my breasts.

"Do you want to touch me, Hunter?"

He nodded. "Yeah, baby."

I shoved down my shirt and moved my bra out of the way so he could massage my breast. Hunter pinched my nipple between his fingers, then dipped down to kiss my lips. Our tongues tangled like we were trying to win a war against the other. Like our bodies both loved and hated the idea of us together because mine did.

Breathing hard, Hunter came in my hand. "Dammit, Grace. Look what you made me do."

"You chose to defy Cole. I didn't make you do anything."

He licked his lips and tucked himself back into his pants. "I can't resist you. It was easier when you were in another state."

I walked toward the bathroom. "Go find me a uniform, Hunter."

"Yes, ma'am," he joked with laughter in his tone.

As I washed the evidence of our encounter from my hand, I stared into the mirror. Hunter was right. I looked like shit. My blonde hair was a tangled disaster in desperate need of shampoo and a flat iron. Sweat streaked my skin, creating a thin layer on my forehead, cheeks, and chest.

How did Hunter get off to me looking like this? *Men.* They could get turned on by the wind blowing just right.

I couldn't attend my first official All Hands ceremony looking like a dog left out in the rain. After washing my face, I dried my skin with a towel and joined Hunter by my bed. He stood next to the window and glanced down at the courtyard.

I cleared my throat, and his eyes met mine. "What are you still doing here? I have to get showered and dressed before the ceremony."

He stepped toward me. "Uniforms are scarce. I can get you one for today, but you'll need to make up with Cole to get replacements."

"I can tell Mark what the cadets did."

Hunter shrugged. "Do whatever you want. If you get our platoon docked points from the Command Cup, the cadets will make your life hell."

"Cole barely looks at me. How do you suggest I butter him up?"

"You can bribe him," he said with a wink.

I snorted. "Please, Cole isn't as easy as you. He'd

rather have blue balls every day for the rest of the year than do me any favors."

"Try talking to him," he suggested. "Maybe you can work your Jedi mind tricks on him."

"Not a chance."

Hunter removed a contraband cell phone from his pocket and stared at the screen. "You better get your sexy ass in the shower. I'll leave the uniform on your bed."

"I'm not getting in the shower with the door unlocked."

"Everyone's in the courtyard, smoking and taking bets on who will win the War Games this year."

"Okay," I agreed. "But come right back."

After he left, I grabbed my toiletry bag and headed into the bathroom. I felt uncomfortable stripping with the hallway door unlocked. So I flipped the lock on the bathroom door and ripped off my dirty clothes, throwing them into a pile on the floor. The knobs groaned as I turned on the water. Then the pipes banged, and a rotten egg scent filled the small space.

When was the last time someone used the water in here? Based on the overwhelming stench, I assumed it had been years. It would take a while to work that smell out of the water, but I didn't have time to let it run until it faded.

I slid the shower curtain to the side, added my hair and body products to the shelves, and then hopped into the stall that desperately needed a good scrub. Even in my disgusting state, I was cleaner than the bathroom.

Thanks for the warm welcome, First Platoon.

I lathered my hair with shampoo and rinsed it with the egg-scented water. Keeping my mouth closed, trying not to take too many breaths, I finished my hair, then moved to my body. It was the shortest shower I'd taken in my life and the least refreshing. When I was reasonably clean, I turned off the water and wrapped my body in a scrap of a towel that had seen better days.

Compared to the rest of the school, with its pristine shine and top-of-the-line everything, it was as if they had forgotten this room existed. Like they'd given me this room to show me how much I didn't belong here. I wrung my hair out and toweled the water off my body. As promised, Hunter followed through with our deal and left a fresh uniform on the bed.

"Hello, Grace," a familiar male voice boomed from the corner of the room.

I gasped at the sight of my least favorite person on the planet, who lounged against the wall like his broad shoulders were holding it up.

"What are you doing in here?"

Hunter

I stole a uniform from one of the smaller cadets and
left it on Grace's bed while she was in the shower.
That girl had worked her way under my skin a long
time ago. She was an itch I needed to scratch, the only
girl I could never shake.

Cole had claimed her for himself when we were in
high school. It wasn't long before I'd convinced him we
could share. Grace Hale was sweeter than any choco-
late, greater than all of my sins.

But I hated betraying Cole.

After a month of not speaking to her, it felt good to
have her pressed against me, her hand working me
over like a pro. Even with her body slick with sweat
and dirt, she was still the prettiest girl I'd ever touched.

Cole made me promise I would help him get rid of
Grace, but I couldn't do that to her. Even if she hadn't
offered sex for favors, I still would have helped her.
That was the reason I went to her room while Cole
was busy with platoon duties.

On my walk back to the apartment I shared with
my friends, guilt ripped through my chest. I knew Cole

had a valid point. He pushed Grace away to keep her safe. It was for her protection. She was too important to the Founders, and now that John Hale was dead, she was vulnerable to even more threats on her life.

Cole waited for me in the hallway outside of our room, arms crossed over his chest. He looked insane, his nostrils flared, eyes wide and full of rage. "Where were you?"

"Dealing with recruits." I avoided his gaze so he couldn't read the lie on my face.

He closed the distance between us, blocking my path. "Was Grace one of those recruits?"

"Leave her alone, Cole."

I rushed past him and headed into the apartment. Brax was in his room with the door open, lying on his bed with an illegal phone in his hand. Other students had to wait until Sundays to use the phone. Not us. Rules didn't apply to anyone in Cole Marshall's inner circle.

The commandant's son was untouchable.

Our apartment accommodated four cadets, but Cole had gotten our former roommate kicked out of the academy at the end of the last term. I had suggested we move Grace into the vacant room to protect her from the other cadets.

That was a non-starter with Cole.

With her dad out of the picture, The Lucaya Group would try to pick us off one by one to get to her.

95

We couldn't trust anyone at this school. And yet, Cole had his head shoved so far up his ass he couldn't see what he was doing to Grace.

Cole followed me into my bedroom, breathing down my neck like he was my asshole dad. "Were you with Grace?"

I spun around to face off with him. "So what if I was?"

"We had a deal."

"No, you set the terms. I agree with your dad. She needs to be with us."

"My dad is wrong about this." Teeth clenched, he shook his head. "Grace is safer away from here."

"She's alone now that John is dead. But she's always had us. We are the closest thing she has to family, and I'm not abandoning her."

"I knew you couldn't last." He sneered at me. "So weak. You take one look at her and fold like a cheap chair."

"I hated ignoring her for the past month."

Cole tipped his head back and laughed. "Listen to yourself, Hunter. I didn't realize you were so in love with Grace."

"I care about her. So do you."

"Which is why she needs to leave." He breathed in my face. "It was easier when John was alive, and she moved all the time. There was no way for The Lucaya Group to reach her."

Before I could get in another word, the front door slamming pulled my attention toward the living room. I poked my head out the door, surprised to find a stranger in our apartment with a black duffel bag slung over his shoulder. He looked lost, not even dressed in uniform, and clearly misinformed about his room assignment.

Cole pushed past me and raced into the living room. "Get out."

"I live here." The dark-haired guy held up a piece of paper and waved it in the air with a cocky grin. "It says so right here."

Cole snatched the paper out of his hand, reading it with his top lip quivering. As if he hadn't already looked out of his mind before, now he looked down-right possessed.

"This is a clerical error." Cole shoved the room assignment at his chest. "The residence hall supervisor will sort it out for you."

"No, I'm not going anywhere."

"Julian, was it?" Cole cocked his head at him. "Since you're new to YMA, I'll give you a free pass. This room belongs to the officers. You hold no rank at this school and are not even a cadet. As I said, it was a clerical error." He waved a dismissive hand, then turned his back on him. "You can go now."

"I might be new here," Julian challenged, moving toward Cole, which forced me to block his path. "My rank was transferrable from Blackwell Military Academy." When Cole turned around, Julian stared at his insignia and smirked. "I see we hold the same rank, Colonel."

Cole clenched his teeth so hard I thought his jaw would snap from the pressure. "There's only one colonel in First Platoon. And you're looking at him."

"Afraid of a little competition, Marshall?"

Cole snarled at him. "Never."

"Yeah, I know who you are," Julian fired back. "I did my research before I transferred."

"Why did you leave BMA in your final year?" I asked him.

"Last minute decision," he said with a shrug. "YMA is a little more progressive if you know what I mean."

"No, we don't fucking know what you mean," Cole hissed.

"I heard you have a girl within your ranks."

Cole's gaze shot to me, then back to Julian. If he overreacted, it would only let Julian know Grace was special to us.

"So what," Cole said with a flippant attitude.

"She's the commandant's new recruit."

Cole's jaw ticked. "Don't act like you know my family. And don't get too comfortable, Archer. I'll have you gone by the end of the day."

Julian tipped his head back and laughed. "I'd like to see you try, Marshall."

"What the fuck is going on out here?" Brax asked from the entryway to his bedroom, scratching his jaw.

"Dealing with an unwanted pest," Cole told him.

Brax's eyes widened at the sight of Julian. "Who the fuck are you?"

"He was just leaving," Cole snapped.

"No, he wasn't." Julian raised his hand to greet Brax. "Julian Archer. Just transferred from BMA."

Brax ignored Julian's extended hand and rolled his eyes. "BMA? Bunch of fucking pussies."

Julian laughed off his comment. "So, which room is mine?"

Cole pointed at the front door. "Leave."

Julian lifted his duffel from the floor and stepped into the vacant room at the front of the apartment. "Nah, I think I'll stay."

I clutched Cole's shoulder to stop him from running after the newbie. "Let's see how this plays out."

"My dad didn't mention anyone transferring from another school… or bunking with us."

"Something's not right. Did you notice his interest in Grace?"

Cole nodded.

"We need to change plans."

His teeth glided across his bottom lip as he thought over my suggestion. "She needs to go."

"She needs to stay."

"Fine," he grunted. "But I'm not easing up on her. If she wants to stay at YMA, she has to earn her place."

"I didn't ask you to go easy on her. Just give her a break. Stop being such a dick." I slid my arm across the back of his neck and pulled him closer. "She needs us, Cole. Grace won't last a week without our help."

"You already broke our agreement. I know you snuck into her bedroom with a new uniform. So what did you get in return?"

"Nothing."

"Please, I've known you since kindergarten. You always have a goal in mind."

I dragged my thumb across my lips. "A gentleman doesn't kiss and tell."

He punched me in the stomach. "Fucker. I hate your ass right now."

"You're just jealous because I had our girl's sexy hands all over me."

Cole rolled his eyes. "I'm not jealous."

"The fuck you're not. You haven't been with anyone since Grace. Maybe you should grovel and beg her to forgive you."

He ended the conversation by walking away, slamming his bedroom door so hard it shook the floor.

"What the fuck was that about?" Brax asked from the kitchen.

I glanced over my shoulder. "Cole needs to get laid."

"Don't we all," Brax deadpanned before pounding an energy drink.

"We have worse problems than getting laid." I grabbed a bottle of water from the refrigerator and leaned against the center island. "Like the asshole who just moved into our apartment."

"And the fine piece of ass down the hall," he said with a wink.

Grace

s I walked out of the bathroom, a familiar male voice said, "Hello, Grace."

I couldn't see him at first.

Then he stepped out from the corner of the room, dressed in his uniform. Navy blue trousers hung low on his narrow hips, the matching blazer open with his shirt untucked. He wore the required gold tie that hung loosely around his neck. Preston Carter looked like a model pretending to be a cadet.

Gorgeous beyond words, he had a straight nose, angular jaw, and kissable lips. But his looks couldn't make up for his shitty personality or the fact he was a no-good lying scumbag. What started as a dance led to a passionate kiss that swept me off my feet. Our relationship started as fast as it ended, and by the time I knew what hit me, I found him cheating on me with a girl from Devil's Creek.

"What are you doing in here, Preston?"

"Came to see how you're settling into the academy."

"Did you mess up my room?"

He lifted his strong shoulders, though his face didn't give away much. "What made you think you would survive a second at this school?"

"Because I didn't grow up with a silver spoon in my mouth and nannies to wipe my ass. Unlike you, I've experienced real military life. This sanctuary for rich boys is nothing."

He shoved off from the wall, slowly approaching me with a grin tugging at his mouth. "You talk a good game, Hale. But let's see how long you last without your boyfriends here to defend you."

"They're not my boyfriends."

"You're a whore. A plaything for the guys to pass around. Do you think you're special to Cole and Hunter?" He shook his head. "They're the ones who told the cadets to fuck up your room."

Tears burned my eyes, threatening to spill, but I wouldn't let them. I had to stay strong, put on a happy face, pretend like I could handle anything. Deep down, I knew I could endure more than most girls my age. But I also had doubts about surviving this place when everyone hated me, when they were working together to get rid of me.

"Get out, Preston." I pointed at the door. "I have to get changed for the ceremony."

"Go ahead. Nothing I haven't seen before."

His lustful gaze traveled up and down my bare thighs, the rest of my body barely covered by the tiny scrap of towel. I'd have to make a lot of deals with Hunter and Cole to restock this place. I needed cleaning supplies, flat paint, new sheets, and a pillow that wasn't torn to shreds if I wanted to pass inspection. They had me right where they wanted me, entirely at their mercy.

I grabbed the uniform Hunter left on the bed and turned my back on my idiotic ex-boyfriend.

"Aww, why so shy, princess?" Preston said in a snarky tone. "You never had a problem showing off your tits and ass."

"Fuck off," I said before I entered the bathroom and locked the door.

By the time I dressed and fixed my hair, Preston left. But I had a feeling this wouldn't be the last time he tried to mess with me.

This was only the beginning.

I SAT in the third row at Marshall Hall. My uncle Mark gave a speech to Alpha Company about the origins of York Military Academy, his family's early investment into the school, and what he had planned for the future.

All eyes snapped to me when he mentioned the

female cadet program that would allow women to attend starting next semester. My cheeks flushed with heat. It was as if their eyes were laser beams searing through my skin. I felt everyone watching me, burning a hole through my back.

On Monday morning, I would start my first day of training. Eight long weeks of physical and mental torture before I could become a cadet. My dad had told me the Marine Corps boot camp was the hardest thing he'd ever endured. That even after close to thirty years in the service, he could still recall every lesson he'd learned over those thirteen weeks at Parris Island. I had a feeling I would one day say the same thing about my training.

I spotted a dark-haired cadet sitting next to Cole on the stage. They both wore the same insignia on their epaulettes. That was odd. Ranks at this school were not the same as the military. They only promoted one person to cadet colonel each year, and that person served as the platoon commander until graduation.

So who was the new guy?

And why did he keep staring at me?

Tall and handsome, he had a baby face and pouty lips that were kind of sexy. He wasn't as hot as Cole or as muscular as Hunter, but he was still pretty tempting.

Cole sat ramrod straight, casually shooting daggers at the new guy, who ate up Cole's hatred. An evil grin tipped up the corners of his mouth. He was enjoying

Cole's anger way too much, and Cole would definitely make him pay for it.

After Mark finished his speech, he asked the incoming students to stand. The guy to my left brushed his fingers on my thigh. I inched to my right to get away from the creep beside me. The men at the school were downright assholes or perverts, with nothing much in between.

We raised our right hands and repeated after Mark to complete the Cadet Oath, which kicked off cadet training. I let my eyes wander across the stage and found Cole glaring at me. He looked so severe, especially dressed in his uniform. His muscles bulged beneath the navy blue jacket with the gold crest on the right pocket.

The ceremony ended a few minutes later.

I filed out of the auditorium with the other recruits, keeping my eyes on the boy in front of me. On the outside, I wanted the cadets to see my stony demeanor. To think I was unaffected by the extra attention the student body was giving me. Mark's speech made the target on my back even bigger. It was like a flashing sign hanging above my head that said, *Bully me.*

I expelled the air from my lungs once I stepped outside. Someone slapped their big palm on my back, rocking me forward. I threw out my arms to find my balance, and then strong arms wrapped around my middle, pressing my back to a hard chest.

"Whoa there, beautiful. We can't have you face planting on your first day."

I glanced up at the handsome face that belonged to the hands that captured me.

"Get your fucking hands off her," Cole shouted.

I stepped out from his embrace and turned around to look at Cole. "He stopped me from falling."

But if he hadn't tapped me on the back like I was one of the guys, I wouldn't have needed his help.

"You." Cole pointed a long finger at the cadet who sat on the stage with him. "Stay away from her."

"Your family might own the school," he shot back. "But you don't own the students." Then he extended his hand to me. "I'm Julian Archer. And you must be Grace Hale."

I shook his hand, but not without Cole grunting his disapproval. "Nice to meet you, Julian."

"Grace," Cole said with a warning in his tone.

"What now, Cole? Am I not allowed to talk to anyone on campus?"

"You can talk to whomever you want."

I moved my hands to my hips and frowned. "But not him?"

Cole's eyes narrowed into slits. "Don't test me, Hale."

Now we were back to Hale like I was just another cadet under his command. He was so damn confusing he gave me whiplash.

Julian held out his hand. "Can I walk you to the mess hall?"

I slipped my fingers between Julian's, and my skin crackled with electricity. "See ya around, Marshall," I said before turning my back on Cole.

Cole

She was a distraction I didn't need, a girl thrown into my life to disrupt the balance and fuck with my head. But that didn't stop me from wanting her.

Throughout dinner, I had to sit back and watch Grace get comfortable with Julian Archer. The new addition to my platoon. Why did the board of directors place him with us?

Arrogant and entitled, he stormed into my apartment like a fucking hurricane, wrecking everything in his path. He was slowly infecting everyone around us with his fake charm and bullshit stories. I could see right through his carefully curated veneer.

He was a liar.

A murderer.

A fraud.

I couldn't find a single thing online about anyone named Julian Archer. No social media profiles. No record he existed. Only links to articles written by someone from Blackwell Military Academy.

A cadet claimed Julian left the academy under interesting circumstances. The school said Julian transferred to pursue other endeavors, which meant he'd done something horrible and was the son of someone important. According to the cadet's blog, the school asked Julian to leave because he was the suspect in a murder investigation. No one filed formal charges against him.

I leaned back in my chair and studied the lying prick. After the way I'd been acting, Grace would never believe me if I told her the truth. Not until I could confirm Julian had done something wrong. The blog was my only evidence and not a credible source of information.

For all I knew, the person who wrote the article had a grudge against Julian and wanted to slander her reputation.

I glanced down the row at Grace. She looked happy, with a smile that reached her beautiful blue eyes. Watching over Grace was one of my favorite things to do. Maybe I was a little obsessed with her, possessed by her. She didn't know how much of an effect she had on me.

After my mother's murder, I couldn't take any chances with Grace. Her life was too important. It was better for her to hate me than for her to get too close.

Without John Hale, she was vulnerable.

She only had us.

The Founders.

The Knights.

Hunter, Brax, and me.

Her arm bumped against Julian's on the table as she threw her head back and laughed. He whispered into her ear, and she smiled so wide it illuminated her face. She used to laugh like that with me. Hell, she used to look at me the same way, too.

She hated me.

But not Hunter.

Or the newbie.

I was the one who made the sacrifice, and yet I paid the highest price—losing Grace. She still flirted with Hunter when she didn't think I noticed, and he returned her gestures. The fucker only made it one month before he folded. And he only lasted that long because Grace was in Virginia.

Brax laid his hand on my arm. "So, what are we doing about the new guy?"

"My PI is looking into his past."

"You think he killed his roommate?"

I shrugged. "Only one way to find out."

"I'm sure your dad and the board of directors looked into his past. They wouldn't have let him come to YMA and keep his rank if the police hadn't cleared him."

"I stopped by my dad's office earlier," I said between bites of food, keeping my voice low. "He's refusing to see me and won't take my phone calls."

"Do you think we should get the Knights involved?"

I shook my head. "Not yet. But if I don't get some answers soon, I'll call the Salvatores. See if they can help us track down information about Julian, the Archers, and the dead cadet."

Brax's eyes widened. "The police ruled it an accident."

"Yeah, but the school hasn't closed the investigation. You know what that means. We do the same shit at YMA."

"No one has died on our watch."

"That you know about."

He lifted an eyebrow. "What are you talking about?"

"Ten years ago, one of the Founders' sons killed someone."

His elbow bumped into mine as our shoulders touched. "Which one?"

"Can't say. The school covered it up." I set the fork on my plate and finished chewing before I added, "The police closed the investigation. They said it was an accident. I only know he was a Founder."

"Who did he kill?"

"A scholarship student."

Grace's laughter cut through the noise in the room, and it was all I could hear. The rest of the room disappeared around her—because I could only see her.

Fuck, I wanted her so badly. We hadn't been together since the summer when we made the sex tape with Hunter.

I wanted to touch her flawless skin, feel her toned thighs. Even with her dressed in an oversized men's uniform, my cock still got rock hard when she swayed her narrow hips.

Brax followed my line of sight and licked his lips. "When are you gonna let me get in on that?"

"What?"

"You know what, Marshall. Why does Hunter get to fuck her, and I don't?"

"If you can get Grace to fuck you, go right ahead. She's all yours."

He glared at me from beneath his dark brows. "Neither of you are supposed to touch her."

"I tried to follow the Founders rules… Not like you would understand."

From eleven years old, I knew Grace was it for me. I had a massive hard-on for her. Grace didn't know her best friend got a boner every time she touched his arm. It wasn't until she turned fourteen that we couldn't deny our feelings.

She wanted to kiss.

I wanted to fuck.

So I waited until she was ready.

Two more years had passed before we took each other's virginity. We were both sixteen, and I was tired of Hunter giving me shit for being the last of our friends to lose my virginity.

But she was worth it.

Every single second.

"She's too perfect," Brax said with hunger in his eyes. "A girl like that needs to be broken in."

A smirk turned up the corner of my mouth. "Already did that."

"Are you serious? I can have her?"

I slapped him on the back. "What's mine is yours."

Brax flashed one of his golden boy smiles. "We're all going to Hell for this."

"One night with Grace is worth it."

Since we were in kindergarten, I'd been friends with Hunter and Brax, fighting over GI Joe's and Lego blocks. We went to Astor Prep together until we were twelve years old, then to York Military Academy. We were in the same platoon, on the same team, and took the same classes.

We shared everything.

So, if Brax wanted Grace, I wouldn't deny him, though I had for a long time.

Because I was an asshole.

And possessive of Grace.

"Any takers on who can break the new girl first?" Rhys Vanderbilt asked.

Grayson Whittaker stuffed a hundred-dollar bill

into Rhys's palm, then glanced around the table. "Who else wants in on this?"

Brax tapped my arm. "Are you going to stop them?"

I stared at the idiots taking bets. "Nope."

"C'mon, bro," he groaned. "Rhys will do anything to win the bet."

And he meant anything. Rhys was a dirty mother-fucker who would use any means necessary to win.

"I'm well aware," I shot back.

"I thought you were just fucking with Grace," Brax said with disappointment in his tone. "So did Hunter. You can't let them take bets on her."

"Why not? We do it all the time. It's not like any of them will get into her pants."

He drew a breath from between his teeth, shaking his head. "Hunter was right. You've lost your fucking mind."

I reached into my back pocket and stood up to throw money into the center of the table, right on top of a stack of bills.

Rhys looked up at me with a sinister grin. "You sure you want in on the action, Marshall?"

I nodded.

"He can't play," Stan Waters hissed. "She's his girl. Unfair advantage."

"Hale is not my girl. If anyone is out of the running, it's Preston."

Brax gave me a look that said, *What the fuck are you doing?*

"Not like it matters." Rhys sneered. "She'll be sucking all of our cocks by the end of the week."

My blood felt like it was boiling inside my veins. I had a plan. Whether it was a good one remained unseen. Brax thought I was throwing Grace to the wolves. Quite the opposite. Because if I were the first to break her, she would be mine.

Untouchable.

A War Games prize.

"Give us until the end of the month," Stan countered. "She won't break that easily."

I looked over at Grace, and my stomach twisted into knots. For her sake, I had to do this. "She only acts like a good girl," I told the group.

Rhys scratched the corner of his jaw, a wicked grin plastered on his face. "Which will make this even more fun."

My end of the table howled like a pack of wolves, loud and wild and out of fucking control. It was a recipe for disaster when you put men with too much money and time on their hands together.

"We'll start this weekend at the bonfire," Rhys suggested. "See how much the plebe can handle."

"What are the terms?" Stan Waters asked.

"You can bet on yourself, or you can pick one of us

to win," Rhys said with a smirk. "Once you pick, you have to stick with it unless you make another wager."

Rhys looked in his element, surrounded by the other cadets who craned their ears to listen. Like a king lording over his subjects. If I weren't the platoon commander, Rhys would have been running this place. He had enough money, power, and connections to topple a small country. And when he put his mind to a goal, he went for it without mercy.

I had to save Grace from these spoiled assholes. But I also couldn't lay down the law and claim her for myself. Not without winning the bet.

Rhys rested his elbows on the table, his gaze sweeping over the group. "Whoever fucks her first wins."

"We need proof," Waters demanded.

"Film it," another suggested.

"I don't care how you prove it," Rhys said. "Just make sure you have evidence of the deed."

Pain shot through my chest at the thought of anyone having sex with her. Hunter and Brax were the exceptions to every rule.

Grayson stretched his long arms out in front of him and winked. "Happy hunting, boys."

Grace

I laughed for the first time in weeks. It almost felt unnatural, like it was something I had forgotten how to do before I met Julian. Not only was he insanely gorgeous, but he was sweet and funny.

He used humor to fill the void and hide what was going on around him. I'd met plenty of Julian's over the years.

Hunter was just like him.

He had a shitty home life, so I understood why Hunter hid at York Military Academy, far away from his controlling father and whore mother. His parents were a complete disaster, not exactly good role models. From what Julian had told me, he had an equally disastrous relationship with his family.

Julian told me another joke, a dirty one this time. I almost choked on the last bite of mashed potatoes and set the fork on my plate.

"What's your deal, Julian Archer? Why did you transfer from a rival military academy in your final year?"

His expression turned grim for a moment, and

then he slapped a crooked grin back on his handsome face. "Not much to tell. My dad runs the largest oil company in the world. He spends most of his time overseas, which meant I got shipped off to a boarding school in England when I was nine."

"You don't have a British accent."

"I was born in the States and have dual citizenship. My dad was working in London, and I'd just chased away the third nanny that year. He was sick of my behavior. So he thought it would straighten me out."

"Did it?"

He shook his head, laughing. "Not even close. After he sent me away, I did anything to get kicked out of school, so I could come home."

"I take it that didn't work."

"Nope. My dad whooped my ass and then shipped me to another school. I'm surprised he didn't run out of places to send me. Money talks. You can do pretty much anything if you have enough of it."

"I wouldn't know," I confessed. "My dad was career military."

"Oh," he said with enthusiasm. "A military brat. You're probably one of the few people at this school that realizes this place is fucking bullshit. YMA is nothing like Annapolis or West Point."

"No, it's not. I visited Annapolis with my dad when I was in high school. I was thinking about applying to USNA, then changed my mind."

"What changed it?"

I rolled my shoulders against the chair. "I don't know. I guess I realized the military wasn't the right career path for me. Do you ever feel like you're supposed to do something just because your dad wants you to do it?"

He nodded. "All the time. So I do the opposite."

"Then how come you're here? You're an adult. College isn't mandatory."

"Same reason as you."

I peeked up at him, surprised by his retort. "I haven't told you my reason."

"I'm looking for answers," he said as if it were a normal response.

I lifted an interested eyebrow. "And you think that's why I'm here?"

"Why else would you be here?"

"To get an education."

He snorted with laughter. "Good luck finding one here. This school exists solely for rich men to teach their sons a lesson."

"And daughters," I corrected. "If I pass cadet training, women will start next semester."

"Which is why they'll never let you pass."

"I'm not easily scared."

"I'm not trying to scare you, Hale. Just stating a fact." He motioned down the table to where the cadets gathered around Cole. His friends exchanged money, a pile of bills at the center of them. "What do you think they're doing right now?"

"Betting on something."

"On you," he said in a deep tone that sent shivers down my arms.

"I doubt that," I countered.

He glared at the cadets at the end of the table. "I don't. You better watch you back, girl." Then he glanced down at me. "In fact, let me watch it for you."

"Are you hitting on me, Archer?"

He smirked. "Either you have little experience with men, or you don't know many nice people."

"A bit of both."

"We're outsiders." He rested his arm on the back of my chair. "Maybe we can help each other out."

"How can I help you when everyone hates me?"

"*Au contraire*," he said in a fake French accent. "I hold the same rank as Marshall. Technically, we should have to compete for one of us to keep it, and yet the board of directors and the commandant let me keep it."

"So Cole didn't lose his rank."

"That would be my guess," he mused, his gaze on the cadets taking bets, laughing and yelling at each other like animals. "Your boy wants me gone. I bet he'd do just about anything to get rid of me."

"Welcome to the club. Cole doesn't want me here, either. No one does."

He tapped my shoulder with his fingers. "I want you here."

"You're either brave or stupid."

"I like to think I'm stupidly brave." Julian consumed the space between us, invading my senses with his manly cologne, and lowered his voice. "So, what's up with you and Marshall?"

"Nothing."

I stuffed food into my mouth to avoid answering questions about Cole.

"I call bullshit. He's obsessed with you."

"Not quite. Cole hates my guts."

"From the deepest desires often come the deadliest hate." His eyebrow tipped up. "For real. What's the story with you and Marshall? Did you date?"

"Our dads were best friends. And until a few months ago, Cole was my best friend."

"What happened?"

I shrugged, unsure of the real reason he pushed me away. "His mom died, and he stopped talking to me. But I know there has to be more than that."

"Do you want to make him jealous?"

I scoffed at the idea. "Cole Marshall doesn't get jealous."

Julian rubbed up against me and winked. "He will if you come with me to the party this weekend."

"My invite must have gotten lost in the mail," I deadpanned, flicking my hair over my shoulder.

"You're coming with me to the party."

"I'm not going as your date," I clarified.

He dipped his head down, and his breath ghosted my earlobe. "Would that be such a bad thing?"

I caught dirty looks from the other cadets at our table and cringed. One of them whispered whore. Another called me a barracks bunny.

Assholes.

"I don't know," I muttered. "I have a target the size of Texas on my back. Thank you for the invite, but I think I'll pass."

"Friends can drink together, right?"

"Friends," I added for extra measure.

He nodded to confirm.

"Okay, I'll come with you. But if you're playing me or working with the other cadets, I'll rip off your balls and keep them in a jar on my nightstand as a souvenir."

He cleared his throat and laughed. "Such brutality for someone so beautiful."

"You better watch out, Julian. This rose has very sharp thorns."

Julian grinned with delight. "I'm counting on it."

I MADE it through the night without getting murdered. Overall, I considered my first night at York Military

Academy a smashing success. Everyone still hated me. Breakfast, lunch, and dinner were awkward as fuck. But at least now I had Julian, who seemed to keep the haters at bay.

Cole hadn't sent his buddies after me.

Even Preston kept his distance.

I figured it was only a matter of time before the monsters came out to play. All day I had been on edge, anticipating everyone's movements, doing my best to watch my ass when Julian wasn't staring at it. He was protective and so far trustworthy, but he was still a man. One who checked me out whenever he didn't think I noticed.

Around nine o'clock on Saturday, Julian knocked on my door, dressed in black jeans and a short-sleeved tee that showed the definition in his biceps. His clothes molded to his body. Like a stupid girl, I might have taken a second or third look before I composed myself.

Because we were just friends.

Just friends and nothing more.

So I kept telling myself.

"Damn, girl," Julian said as he appraised my outfit. "Looking good. On second thought, maybe we should stay in tonight."

I slid my hands to my hips and shook my head. "Not a chance."

"I may need to hide you from the cadets."

"I'm wearing jean shorts and a tank top." I held out my arms for him to inspect. "Nothing special."

He put his fingers between his lips and whistled. "You look special, alright."

I blushed at his comment and playfully swatted at his chest. "Stop it. People are looking at us."

He glanced over his shoulder to survey the floor with mild curiosity. "They can look all they want," he said a few octaves higher than usual to ensure the boys passing my room heard him. "But they're not allowed to touch."

"Julian." I rolled my eyes. "Saying things like that will only make them want to fuck with me more."

"Sweetheart, they want to fuck you. Not fuck *with* you."

After I locked the door and stuffed the key into my pocket, I left Bryant Hall with Julian. I tried to ignore the evil gazes aimed at me. The whispers of the students followed us like smoke in the wind.

We took Walker Pass, the main pathway that ran through the center of the campus until we reached the tennis court. Droves of students rushed past us with cases of beer and liquor bottles in their hands. I wondered how they got alcohol on the premises when we couldn't have a cell phone. But these rich pricks always got what they wanted.

By the looks of it, most of the school was at the beach for the bonfire. Rock music blared from a distance and people shouted. A bright fire blazed through the woods. How would they pull this off without getting caught?

"I bet the winter months get real sad and desperate around here."

"Good thing you have me watching your back, woman. You're a sitting duck at this school." His eyes traveled up and down the length of my body. "And when you dress like this." He shook his head. "Kinda hard to focus when I look at you."

Julian stopped at the edge of the woods and peeled back a thick leafy encasement. He gestured for me to go ahead of him. I ducked below a low-hanging branch, using the fire as my guide, and walked beside Julian. Cadets rushed past us in a hurry, my name a whisper on their lips. The knot in my stomach twisted as I moved through the woods.

A crisp breeze blew off the water, causing my teeth to chatter. Julian hooked his arm around my back, and I tensed for a moment, now all too aware of his hard body pressed against mine.

"It's okay. I won't bite," he said with a grin.

I wanted him to bite me.

Was that such a bad thing?

We followed the loud voices ahead of us, maintaining a safe distance from the others as we navigated the hiking trail. The party was in full swing on the beach, fires raging, the drinks flowing. Dozens of men appraised my body, and I felt the heat of their gazes everywhere.

Cole stood around the fire with Hunter and Brax at his sides. When his eyes landed on me, he greeted me with one of his cold, angry stares that sliced into my chest. One look, and the bastard held my damn heart captive. Arms crossed over his chest, Hunter shifted his weight beside Cole, his intense gaze on me. Beside him, Brax studied me as he drank beer from a plastic cup.

It hurt that I would never have them again, that they were drawing lines between us. Well, I'd never had Brax, though there were a few times over the years when something almost happened between us.

Multiple bonfires raged on the beach. A group of students huddled around the smaller one that blazed in the darkness, illuminating their faces. Preston stretched his long legs out on the sand with his arm rested on a log. He sat with one leg bent as he took a sip from his beer. Dressed in black designer shorts and a gray button-down shirt with the sleeves rolled up to his elbows. As usual, he looked calm and casual, like he didn't have a care in the world.

His eyes burned holes through my clothes, and I didn't miss the way he breathed deeper, his chest rising and falling. He still wanted me. That much was evident when he showed up in my room uninvited.

Julian grabbed my hand and steered me toward the

group. Hunter rested his boot on top of the cooler with a beer in hand.

"Hey," I said to Hunter.

Cole just stared, like we were having a contest to see who would blink first. He was so intense sometimes. Hunter grabbed two beers from the cooler and handed them to Julian and me.

Brax sipped from his beer, inspecting every inch of my body. "You still doing the Capoeira routine I showed you?"

His mom was Brazilian and had lived there until she met his dad and moved to the United States. She owned a studio in Devil's Creek that focused on Capoeira, a martial art that combined dance and acrobatics.

I glanced up as he moved in front of me. With his tanned skin and dark features, he was the complete opposite of Cole, but he was just as tempting.

"Is this your idea of flirting, Brax?"

He shoved a hand through his dark brown hair that had a slight curl. "Just making conversation with a beautiful woman."

I drank from the cup. "To answer your question, yes."

Brax slid his lip between his teeth, eyeing me up. "I can see that."

"You guys know Julian."

All three of the boys glared at Julian with pure hatred.

"There's way too much testosterone in the air," I commented. "Can you guys take it down a notch?"

"He doesn't belong here," Cole said in a nasty tone. "And neither do you."

"Cole, you're getting on my nerves. Stop with all the macho bullshit."

I reached out to smack his bicep, but he was too fast. In a flash, he had me pinned against his chest, his long fingers digging into my hip, squeezing me so hard I winced.

"Stop it, Cole."

His hand trailed down my side as he breathed on my neck. "No."

"I know you. This isn't like you."

Everyone on the beach stopped to watch the scene play out. Wherever Cole went, he was the center of attention, which didn't bode well for me. I was already Enemy Number One at this school. Maybe I should have gone with my gut instinct and stayed in my room.

Alone.

Where no one could mess with me.

"Leave her alone, Marshall," Julian commanded with authority.

Red-hot waves of anger radiated off Cole. "Stay out of this, Archer. Learn your place."

Cole wrapped his arm around my stomach. "We need to talk."

"Not when you're acting like an asshole."

Before I could react, Cole lifted me in his arms and threw me over his shoulder like a sack of laundry.

Julian rushed to my side and tugged on Cole's shoulder. "Put her down, Marshall."

Cole laughed, not the least bit deterred. "Fuck off, Archer. You might hold the same rank, but you don't run this school. Marshall Law is the only law that matters."

"I'm not afraid of you. Now, let her go."

"Make me," Cole challenged.

His fingers seared my skin like hot pokers.

"Put me down." I pounded Cole's back with my fist. "Cole, what is your fucking problem?"

I wriggled in his strong arms, inching my way down his chest, so I could kick him in the balls. He groaned, then released his grip on me. Julian caught me before Cole staggered back, holding onto his precious jewels.

"Fucking bitch," Cole muttered.

Julian set my feet on the ground and inspected my face. "You okay?"

I fixed my shirt and shorts back into place. "Yeah, I'm fine."

After Cole composed himself, he stood at his full

height, towering over me. He extended his hand. "We need to talk, Grace."

"I'm not in the mood for talking."

He slipped his fingers between mine and pulled hard. "Let's go."

I shook him off. "No."

Hunter slid his hands to my shoulders from behind and bent down to whisper into my ear. "Go with him. It could make the next year a lot easier for you."

"Unfair advantage," a boy yelled from a distance. "Marshall's a fucking cheater."

I peeked up at Cole and Hunter. "What is he talking about?"

"Come with me." Cole clamped his fingers around my wrist. "And I'll tell you."

I glanced at Julian. "I'll be right back."

"C'mon, Grace," Julian protested. "You can't trust him."

"I've known him for most of my life. He won't hurt me."

I turned my back on Julian and let Cole lead the way, wondering if I was making a horrible decision.

Grace

I followed Cole into the woods. An eerie chill rolled down my arms, my heart slamming into my chest with each step we took away from the beach. Julian was so far away, no longer within my reach.

What was I thinking?

Cole had been acting erratically for a while, and I wasn't sure if I could trust him.

"Where are you taking me?" I asked, forcing down the bile rising from my stomach.

"Not much farther."

Cole's grip tightened on my hand as he led me down the walking trail. After a few minutes, Cole stopped in front of an old chapel. It was rundown, the stained glass windows broken and covered with grime.

"Did you come here to ask God for forgiveness for what you're about to do to me?"

Cole tipped his head back and laughed. "No, Grace. I don't want forgiveness."

The hairs on my arms stood at attention. "Why are we here?"

"To talk."

He inched forward like a hunter, and I took a few steps back, which only put me at a disadvantage. Cole snaked his arm around my middle, pinning me against the tree with his muscular chest.

"You can talk without touching me."

"Maybe I want to touch you, Grace." His lips brushed mine, the heat from his breath awakening the hunger inside me. "Maybe I *need* to touch you."

"Not like this." I pushed on his chest with my palms to create some distance. "You're not acting like the person I know. It's like you're possessed."

"I'm doing this to protect you." He cupped the side of my face with his hand. "To keep you from getting hurt."

"Sure as hell doesn't feel like it. You've done nothing but push me away and make me feel like shit."

"I'm sorry, Grace." He swiped a strand of hair behind my ear. "But I'm doing what I think is best for you."

"How about you let me decide what's best for me?"

"There's so much you don't know." He sighed. "So much I wish I could tell you."

"It's me, Cole. Not some stranger. What's so horrible you can't tell me?"

He rested his forehead against mine, and we stood there in silence, breathing in unison. I forgot about the pain and suffering he'd caused me over the past month. I just wanted my best friend back.

We hadn't been together since we made the sex tape with Hunter. My body ached for him. With every ounce of my being, I needed him to satiate the desire brewing inside me. His hand traveled over the front of my tank top, his fingers grazing the tops of my breasts. I shivered from his touch.

It was too soft, too delicate for Cole.

Cole fisted my hair and pulled my mouth to his. I sucked in a deep breath as our eyes met. The usual hesitation was in his eyes, and that same feeling settled deep into my bones. I wrapped my leg around his back and moaned with each kiss he planted on my neck before making his way up to my jaw.

"What did you want to talk to me about?"

"I don't want to talk," he said against the shell of my ear. "I just wanted to get you alone without your new boyfriend tagging along."

I tilted my head to the side, a whimper escaping my lips. "Julian isn't my boyfriend."

His hand slid over my windpipe. "You need to keep your distance from him."

I shoved his hand away. "No, he's my friend."

"I'm your friend, Grace. I still want to do dirty things to you."

"He's just my friend, nothing more."

His eyes flickered with madness. "So you don't want to fuck him?"

Heart pounding in my chest, I snapped my mouth shut.

"That's what I thought. Stay the fuck away from him."

"Don't tell me what to do."

"He's not who he says," Cole fired back. "Your buddy Julian is a lying murderer."

A flash of heat swept over my body, warming my cheeks. "No, he's not. You're just saying this to get him away from me. Because you don't want me to have any friends."

"What story did he tell you?"

"He said his father is an oil tycoon and travels around the world. That he spent most of his life in boarding schools in Europe."

"He got kicked out of Blackwell Military Academy."

I shook my head, not wanting to hear what could have been the truth about Julian. "He said he transferred."

"When you have enough money, you can make any problem go away. That's what his father did. And I'm going to prove it."

"You're accusing him of murder with no proof? Unbelievable." I stood on my tippy toes and got in his face. "It sounds like you're jealous of Julian and need a reason to hate him. We both know this is about me."

He lifted me, hooking my legs around him, and

pushed me back into the tree. "Fine, maybe I care about him chasing after you."

"Julian isn't chasing me. He's just being my friend. Trying to keep assholes like you away from me."

"He's not doing a good job."

I wiggled in his arms, desperate to break free. "I hate you, Cole Marshall."

"No, you don't." Cole licked my cheek, which was oddly sensual, and made my pulse quicken. "You want this, Grace. Just admit it."

I moaned.

"Say it, brat." His mouth hovered over my ear, sending a ripple of heat down the right side of my body. "You want me. You want this."

Cole was my greatest sin and even bigger weakness. When we were together, I couldn't control myself. So I tugged at the ends of his short hair and kissed him. I rocked my hips to meet his, desperate to create friction between us. His long, hard cock pressed into my belly, and I reached between us to stroke him over the fabric.

He bit my lip, tugging on it with his teeth like an animal. "I see my little brat wants to play."

"I hate you."

"Stop saying that." His eyes met mine. "We both know it's a lie."

"I'm not having sex with you."

He kissed my neck, destroying my will to fight him. "I'd rather lick your pussy."

"Oh, my God, Cole."

He licked the length of my neck, then dragged his teeth along my skin. "God can't save you now."

I glanced over at the nearly crumbling chapel and almost laughed. It was no longer a place of worship, but it still felt wrong to let Cole claim me when I could see the remnants of angels stained on the glass panels. Before I could think too hard about it, Cole's tongue swept into my mouth.

His hand dipped beneath my shirt, moving up my bare stomach and over my lacy bra. He pinched me over the fabric, and I released a whimper. Cole twisted my nipple, this time harder than before, and I squealed.

He sucked the tiny bud into his mouth, giving equal love to my breasts, sucking and biting me until I shivered from the slightest touch.

After a while, Cole set me on the ground.

He gripped my hips, then lowered to his knees in front of me, leaving a trail of kisses down my stomach. Every nerve ending in my body came alive at once. He took his sweet ass time pressing kisses to my skin, savoring every second.

Tired of waiting and desperate for a release, I grabbed his hand and shoved it down the front of my panties. "Cole, please. Stop torturing me."

He winked, an evil grin tugging at the corners of his mouth.

"Make me come already."

His fingers gripped the waistband of my shorts. "Patience," he said in a husky tone.

Cole unzipped my shorts. My heart raced faster than a pack of hungry wolves, beating so loudly I could hear a ringing in my ears. Then, with practiced precision, Cole inched my shorts and panties over my ass, exposing my hot, waxed skin to the chilly air.

"Fuck," he groaned. "You smell so fucking good, brat."

I shivered when his lips brushed the skin right below my belly button. Slow and steady, Cole tasted every bit of my flesh, my body trembling with need. He let my shorts and panties gather around my ankles. I stepped out of them, and then he resumed his place between my thighs.

Cole peeked up at me, his eyes wild with desire. He licked his lips, and then his gaze dropped to my soaking wet pussy. A moment of debate settled on his face before he plunged two fingers inside me. I whimpered, not only from the intense wave of pleasure but because of the brutal way he claimed me. He thrust his fingers like they were his cock, filling me to the hilt.

I tugged on his hair. Then he licked me straight down the middle, and I cried out his name.

He glanced up at me with a devious grin. "Feel good, brat?"

"Yes," I whispered. "Don't stop."

He raised my right thigh over his shoulder, diving deeper with his tongue. I arched my back against the tree, lifting my hips. He devoured me like a starving animal, taking me with brute force. My eyes slammed shut each time he sucked my clit into his mouth, his teeth grazing my sensitive flesh.

He eventually swapped his fingers for his tongue, licking between my slick folds as he rubbed my clit, making circular motions with his thumb. I screamed his name, and with each moan, I pulled his hair harder. That encouraged him to keep going, forcing his tongue to go deeper and deeper until he tasted every inch of me.

I panted as he grabbed my ass cheeks, long fingers digging into my skin as I hit the peak of my climax. His name poured out of my mouth right before my legs shook uncontrollably. One after another, my orgasms spilled out of me in violent waves of passion.

After I came on his tongue, he sat back on his heels and attempted to catch his breath while I did the same.

"Fucking hell, Grace." He wiped his mouth with the back of his hand. "You taste too fucking good."

Laughter spilled from my mouth. "And you're too good at that."

He smirked, then rose to his full height. Cole caged me against the tree as he dipped down to kiss my lips. I reached between us to grab his waistband, and he pushed my hand away.

"Get dressed."

Bending down to collect my shorts from the ground, he tucked my panties into his pocket, and then handed over my shorts.

I grabbed them from him. "Give back my panties."

Cole turned his back to me. "No."

"What kind of game are you playing, Cole?"

He spun around in an instant, leveling me with a heated gaze. "One that keeps you from getting fucked by every cadet at this school."

My mouth opened in horror. "What are you talking about?"

"There's a bounty on your head. The first cadet to claim the prize gets to keep you."

"You used me?" I bit my lip to steady my voice. "What the fuck is wrong with you?"

"Get yourself together, Grace." He walked deeper into the woods, his back to me as he headed toward the beach. "Go back to your room and take a shower."

Waves of anger surged through my veins, igniting a fire beneath my skin. I'd never felt more used in my life. Make her feel good, then steal her panties. What the hell kind of game was he playing with these sick and twisted cadets?

He stormed away without another word.

I wasn't sure what hurt more—my heart or my pride. After I got dressed, I trekked through the woods, unsure of the correct direction. The bonfires had simmered to a golden glow that seemed even farther than before. I lost sight of where I was going because I was too busy crying to pay attention. And that was when I heard the first twig snap a few feet away from me.

Then another.

And another.

Was someone watching me?

Silence fell over the woods. I halted in place, with nothing more than the sound of my heart beating. When I was in high school, my dad sent me to survival camp for a few weeks at the start of the summer. He forced me to learn skills to live on the land, to hunt and kill to survive.

Twigs snapped beneath the weight of something heavy. My heart clambered out of my chest, pounding so hard and fast I couldn't catch my breath. I stood painfully still, craning my ear to listen. And then what sounded like an object hit the ground, rustling the leaves a few feet from me.

"I know you're there," I yelled. "Show your face, you coward."

A moment passed before a figure stepped onto the hiking trail, dressed in all black, a hood covering his face. I took one last look, knowing I was at a disadvantage, and then I ran like hell.

Cole

I won the bet, and I still felt like shit. To keep the others away from Grace, I had to be an asshole, a monster. I had to push her even farther away. She probably hated my guts after the stunt I pulled, and I deserved every bit of her anger.

Hunter waved his hand as I exited the woods, standing at the edge of the beach. Brax stood beside him with a beer in hand. I should have been here with them, drinking and having a good time before the start of our final year. Instead, I was hurting Grace just so the others wouldn't hurt her to win the bet.

"Please tell me you didn't do it," Hunter said with a disappointed look on his face.

"Where is Grace?" Brax asked.

"I told her to go back to Bryant Hall and take a shower."

Hunter shook his head.

"I didn't ask for your opinion or your approval," I told him.

"I can't believe you left her in the woods alone."

Brax leaned into my arm and lowered his voice. "Julian disappeared after you left with Grace."

I narrowed my eyes at him. "Do you think he went after her?"

"No idea." Brax gulped down his beer. "But you're an asshole for leaving her. We don't know Julian or why he's here."

"Or why he's so interested in Grace," Hunter cut in.

"He won't hurt her."

"How can you be so sure?" Hunter said.

"Classes don't start until Monday. If he's planning something, he'll wait until everyone is too busy to notice. Now would be a stupid time to disrupt the status quo."

"Marshall," Rhys called out. "Did you finish the job?"

He sauntered over to the bonfire with a bottle of Jack in hand, dressed like a preppy Ivy League mother-fucker with a massive grin stretching the corners of his mouth. I reached into my pocket, the sweet smell of Grace's pussy clinging to the air like perfume, and handed over her panties.

Hunter's nose tipped up at her scent. Without a doubt, he knew I was telling the truth. Plus, Grace wouldn't have willingly handed over her panties, so I could win a bet. She might hate me for it now, but she would thank me for it later.

I just saved her a world of trouble.

Rhys raised Grace's panties to his nose and took a whiff. "Fuck me. She smells better than I imagined."

I wanted to beat the fucking shit out of him for envisioning anything about Grace. Not even a hair on her head. She was off-limits to Rhys and the other fuckers at this school. It was bad enough Hunter and I had betrayed the oath we'd taken. We'd broken dozens of the Founders' laws by violating Grace's beautiful body.

Like a rare flower or an extinct species, The Devil's Knights protected her. We were doing a shit job because she was too tempting. Too perfect and special and everything I had ever wanted.

We were doomed from the fucking start.

Rhys passed Grace's panties to Grayson, Stan, and the other guys. Even Preston joined the action, grabbing the lace from Max's hand. He'd fucked Grace a few times over the summer, which was what started up my feelings for her again. I let her date Preston when I knew she would rather have me.

We had promised not to cross the line after we'd done it so many times in the past. That was the reason I didn't protest when Grace announced she was dating Preston. She did it to make me jealous, and it worked. I stewed over her decision, unable to watch them together. But when she came to my house, wanting revenge for Preston cheating on her, I couldn't tell her no.

I didn't have the strength to turn her away.

Neither did Hunter.

After everyone got their chance to verify I'd been with Grace, the panties ended up in Rhys's hand. They couldn't deny the scent was fresh and belonged to Grace. She was the only woman on the campus, apart from the administrative staff.

"How do we know you fucked her?" Rhys asked. "She could have given these to you."

"Yeah," a few people groaned.

"We need real proof," Grayson said. "Her panties don't prove shit."

"I have evidence," Preston said with a taunting smirk.

Rhys angled his body to look at him. "Hand it over then."

"No. Don't you dare."

"What's the big deal, Marshall?" Rhys's eyes flickered with excitement. "Afraid of a little competition?"

"Never," I shot back.

"He doesn't want to share his toy with you."

I aimed a nasty look at Preston. "Stay out of this."

Rhys smirked.

"She's not as impressive as Cole thinks," Preston chimed. "I got sick of her after a few weeks."

"Shut your fucking mouth." Hunter hovered over

Preston. "Say another word about Grace, and I'll split open your skull."

"Hunter." I tugged on his arm. "He's not worth it."

I tried to hide my feelings for Grace from the guys. But now that Preston had mentioned that he had evidence of Grace and me, I feared it was only a matter of time before the sex tape came to light.

A moment of silence fell over the group. Waves crashed lightly against the beach, and then a scream sliced through the air. I thought I had imagined it until Hunter's head snapped toward the woods. Then I heard it again, a shrill cry that sounded female.

Grace.

Hunter gave me a worried look. "You shouldn't have left her."

"Don't start with me."

I pushed my way through the group and headed toward the woods, flanked by Brax and Hunter. The other cadets trailed behind. I raced into the thick underbrush, following the sound of Grace's desperate plea.

"Cole," Grace yelled.

I ran in her direction, afraid I wouldn't get to her in time. Hunter and Brax were at my sides, swatting at fallen branches in their way. She sounded so scared, her voice pained. Fuck, this was my fault. If anything happened to her, I would only have myself to blame.

A figure raced toward me, and when the moonlight

hit her face, I let out a sigh of relief. I opened my arms for Grace. Instead of hugging me, she cocked her arm back and punched me in the jaw. My head turned to the side from the power behind her fist. For a small girl, she could hit like a dude. It was all the training John Hale had forced upon her. He wanted to make sure she was ready for any situation.

"You piece of shit." Grace shoved her palms into my chest. "How dare you leave me out here with no fucking panties and then have your idiot friends chase me through the woods?"

A few of the guys behind us laughed.

She pointed a finger at them. "Shut your fucking mouths. I'm not in the mood for any more of your frat-boy bullshit."

"We didn't do anything." Rhys raised his hands in the air. "We were on the beach and heard you screaming."

Grace looked up at me.

"It's true. I came looking for you."

She attempted to punch me again, but this time I was ready and caught her fist in mid-air. I twisted her arm, forcing her to give up.

With an annoyed groan, she shook me off and stepped back, her eyes falling to Hunter. "Is he telling the truth?"

"Yes," Hunter agreed.

"Then who was chasing me?"

"What's going on?" Julian asked.

I turned to my right. "Where the fuck did you go?"

"Back to the dorms," he said with a nonchalant shrug.

"Fucking liar. Someone chased Grace through the woods. You're the only cadet unaccounted for."

"That's bullshit," Julian said. "I ran into dozens of cadets at Bryant Hall. Ask any of them."

I gritted my teeth. "You better hope someone can corroborate your story, Archer."

He held up his hands in surrender. "Chill, Marshall."

"What were you doing at the apartment?"

"Since when is it illegal to take a shit?" Julian glared at me. "And what's all this about?"

"Are you deaf, motherfucker?" Hunter said with fire behind his words. "Someone attacked Grace."

Julian pushed his way past a few of the senior cadets and placed his hand on Grace's shoulder. "Are you okay?"

"No, I'm not fucking okay."

"Get your hands off her," I snapped.

Julian laughed off my command as if I'd just told a joke. With Grace, I didn't fuck around.

Grace shook her head. "You don't own me. I'm not your property."

"So it's true," Rhys said to no one in particular. "You two sealed the deal earlier."

Grace threw her hands onto her hips and addressed the group. "So, what are the terms of the bet?"

"Don't do this, Grace."

"No, Cole. I want to know what was so special that you ruined our friendship over it."

Someone behind me muttered a confused, "Friends?"

"Told you he cheated," another guy mumbled.

"Whoever fucks you first wins," I admitted.

Grace shook her head. "How much is my pussy worth?"

"C'mon, Grace."

I reached out for her, and she swatted at my hand. "I expect this from Preston and Rhys, but not you. I hate you, Cole Marshall. I hate you so fucking much I wish I never met you." Then she looked at Rhys. "And for the record, Cole didn't fuck me. So whatever story he told you was bullshit."

I heard the guys exchange money behind me and cringed. Another bet. They were upping the stakes because I didn't close the deal with Grace. Maybe I should have fucked her when she begged for my cock. But I already felt terrible for deceiving her.

"He's a creep who stole my panties," Grace told Rhys.

"But how did he get them?"

She bit her bottom lip. "He tricked me."

The more she talked, the more she put her foot in her mouth. I squeezed my eyes shut and breathed through my nose. I was doing her a favor by pretending we had sex. So why did she have to say something?

Grace spun around, her back to me, but before she could walk away, I grabbed her shoulder. "Where do you think you're going?"

"To bed." She knocked my hand away. "And don't stop me."

Julian was at her side, dipping down to whisper something into her ear. She nodded, then grabbed his hand. He glanced over his shoulder at me and winked. My blood boiled with rage, surging through my veins.

"Grace, don't trust him."

She halted in place but didn't turn around to look at me. "You're the one I don't trust, Cole. Go fuck yourself."

"Sounds like a lover's quarrel to me," one cadet said.

I groaned. "Shut up. All of you. Go back to the fucking beach and get lost."

Grace

There was a thin line between love and hate, and at the moment, I felt nothing but hatred for Cole. I should have known better. After he ghosted me, I melted in his arms, allowed myself to get wrapped up in his masculine scent, his possessive touch. His tongue, those strong arms…

Ugh, I hate him.

And his sexy ass body.

I walked with Julian back to Bryant Hall. We'd only spoken a few times along the way, mostly because I asked him to give me some time to process. He was good at reading my mood and sensing my emotions. Julian just let me be myself.

Cole used to be that person for me.

As we approached my room, I removed the key from my pocket. "Do you want to come in?"

Julian grinned. "Yeah, I'd love that."

"The place is a mess," I warned.

"That doesn't bother me."

I pushed open the door, revealing the disaster zone.

"Hmm…" He pressed his lips together as his eyes swept over the room. "Need help cleaning?"

"No, I couldn't ask you to do that."

"You're not asking." He followed me into the room and closed the door. "I'm offering. Let me help you."

I sat on the bed that needed a fresh pair of sheets and stared around the room. "It still doesn't feel real."

Julian plopped down beside me. "What doesn't?"

"My dad has been dead for a week, and I keep thinking he's going to show up and say it was all a joke. I know it's not. But there's a part of me that wishes all of this were a dream. That I'll go to bed tonight, and tomorrow I'll go back to my real life."

Julian squeezed my shoulder. "Look, I know what you're going through, Grace. My mom died when I was ten. It was the worst time of my life."

I sniffed back the tears. "How did you adapt?"

"I didn't," he confessed. "Not at first, anyway. I was already at odds with my dad, who couldn't even stand to look at me. And when my mom died, he withdrew from me even more. I won't bullshit you. In my experience, it usually gets worse before it gets better. There is a light at the end of the tunnel. It won't always feel so lonely and dark. But you have to walk through the darkness first."

"I thought I'd be having this conversation with Cole." I sighed at the thought. "We used to be there for each other."

"You guys are that close, huh?"

"We *were* that close until Cole's mom died. After that, he shut me out, told me to lose his number. His behavior hasn't changed. He still hates me."

"I see the way he looks at you," Julian said in Cole's defense.

"What do you see?"

"Desire."

"Wanting to fuck me isn't the same. I need a friend. I need the person he used to be, not someone to give me an orgasm."

"I'm here for you."

"Thank you." I smiled. "I appreciate you sticking out your neck for me. But I feel bad because the cadets will hate you, too."

"I doubt I would have been all that popular, anyway. I have a habit of making enemies at every school."

"Do you do it to piss off your dad? Or did you genuinely hate the people at each school?"

He shrugged. "A little of both, I guess. At first, I started fights to get kicked out, so I could go back home. I hated boarding school."

"And I thought being a military brat was hard. We moved a lot. I never had friends. Only Cole for a long time. Then I met Hunter."

"You're close with both of them?"

I nodded.

Julian tapped his long fingers on my knee, and his eyes lifted to meet mine. He was so adorable with the cutest smirk, a dimple that creased his tanned skin, and green eyes that had a hint of yellow. When he held my gaze for too long, I cleared my throat, needing a distraction from my thoughts.

"So, what was it like living in England?"

"I'm a spoiled American with no clue about English customs or slang. How do you think I adjusted?"

"I lived in Germany with my dad. It wasn't so bad, but we rarely left the base."

"Can you speak German?"

I laughed. "Like two words."

He beamed with excitement. "Okay, let's hear them."

"*Guten Tag*," I said.

"What does that mean?"

"Good day."

"Do you know any other words?"

"*Arschloch*," I said with laughter in my voice.

"That one sounds dirty."

"It means asshole."

"Did you learn anything other than hello and some curse words?"

I shook my head. "Not really. I went to school on the base. Everyone there spoke English. I didn't need to learn the language."

"You'll survive the year," Julian said with certainty.

"I hope so."

"You've been training for this your entire life. Most of the cadets at this school have no real-world experience. That's what separates you from the pack."

A moment of silence swept over the room. I stared at the wall, my thoughts drifting between memories of my old life and new. Maybe Julian was right. I'd been adapting to my environment my entire life.

These cruel cadets tried to break me.

But I would never let them win.

I raised my hand to my mouth and yawned. The weight of the day felt as if it were crashing down on me. With twenty-four hours left until my first day of cadet training, I needed to get some sleep.

"Tired?" Julian asked.

"Yes." I yawned again. "I hate to kick you out."

He shot up from the bed. "I'll see you at breakfast."

I followed him to the door and stood on my tippy toes to wrap my arms around his neck, crushing him with a hug. His arms tightened around me, and our chests pressed together.

He lowered his head, and the heat from his breath fanned across my lips. We were too close, and he smelled too good. His lips moved against mine. He closed his eyes as if he wanted a real kiss. I stood there, painfully still, and let our lips touch, making no move to stop him. After a few seconds, Julian seemed to note my resistance, and his eyes snapped open.

"I'm sorry," I whispered. "I can't. I'm not ready. Not after what happened tonight."

Cole said Julian was a liar. While I didn't think he was the person chasing me, I wasn't sure who had terrorized me. It was too dark. A hood covered the person's face, their body clad in all black.

"It's all good." Julian shrugged. "See ya tomorrow, Hale."

THE FOLLOWING DAY, I ate breakfast with Julian and my platoon. We didn't have to sit in silence on the weekends, so I soaked up my R&R time. After I exercised in my room, I showered and changed into loose-fitting clothes. Thanks to the jerk-off cadets in First Platoon, I wore a pair of sweats that had rips in various places.

Hunter promised to give me another uniform for our brief sexual encounter. But I didn't have laundry detergent or an iron, so I had to rely on Hunter until I could figure out an alternative solution to my clothing problem.

Dozens of cadets sat in the courtyard outside of Bryant Hall. The seniors and juniors seemed to be pretty tight, smoking and yelling and even taking bets.

Of course, Preston held court alongside his buddies, Rhys Vanderbilt and Grayson Whittaker.

When Rhys spotted me, I walked faster, keeping my eyes ahead.

"Where are you going, GI Barbie?" Rhys taunted in a harsh tone. "Come over here and chill with your platoon. We want to get to know you better."

An echo of laughter rolled throughout the space. I stopped dead in my tracks and looked at him. Rhys was gorgeous, and he damn well knew it. He shoved a hand through his black hair and smirked when our eyes met.

"I don't want to know you, Rhys."

His smirk turned into a frown that tugged at the corners of his mouth. Then he patted the open seat on the stone bench beside him. "Get over here, beautiful. I can make your life a lot easier at the academy."

I rolled my eyes. "I'm not interested."

"Oh, c'mon, Hale. You won't survive a week without help."

Grayson slid his thumb across his bottom lip. If I didn't know he was a psychopath, I would find the subtle gesture attractive. But I'd heard enough about Grayson from Cole and Hunter to realize I didn't want to be alone with him.

"I don't need your help," I shot back.

"You're insulting my friend." Preston leaned forward with his elbows rested on his thighs. "Now, be a good little whore and say thank you to Rhys for his charity."

"Thank you, Rhys," Grayson said with laughter in his tone. "It's not that hard to say, Barbie."

Furious, I shook my head. "I don't want or need any favors from the likes of you three. So leave me the fuck alone."

Grayson tapped his thigh with his fingers, staring through me with his hardened gaze. He seriously creeped me out whenever I was in the same room as him. All the guys from the academy had been at Cole's parties over the years. This wasn't the first time I was meeting some of them.

I stood a few feet from their bench, my gaze sweeping down the row of sexy but infuriating cadets. "You want me for the same reason as Preston," I told Rhys. "Because you want what Cole has."

"Cole doesn't want you anymore," Preston said with way too much enthusiasm. "He laid down Marshall Law before you got here. Your boyfriends ordered our platoon to fuck with your shit."

"Tell me something I don't already know."

Rhys extended his hand, and I stared at it as if he had a disease. But when I noticed Cole coming out of Bryant Hall with Hunter and Brax, I wanted them to hurt. I wanted them to feel my pain. So I took Rhys' hand, and he hooked the other around my back, pulling me onto his lap. Bergamot and fresh linen filled my nostrils. It didn't surprise me the rich boy smelled as good as he looked.

"That's a good girl," Rhys whispered in my ear. His hand moved to my hip, and he held me with possession as Cole passed by with his friends. "Marshall and Banks have had you for long enough. It's our turn."

The hurt and anger on Cole's face sparked an inferno inside me. He had no right to give a damn about me talking to another cadet, not after ignoring me for an entire month.

"We can get you new uniforms." Rhys breathed mint across my cheek. "Anything you need."

"I'm sensing a but." I slid off his lap after Cole left with his friends. "And what is the cost of your charity?"

Rhys spread his long legs and grabbed himself over his pants, his grin reaching his eyes. "For starters, you can stop giving me shit and put that pretty mouth to good use."

I laughed. "Go to hell, Rhys."

"She's so mean," he told Grayson. "But fuck, it turns me on."

Grayson nodded his agreement while Preston glared at me. He still wanted to fuck me. That much was evident by the way he undressed me with his eyes. After I sent him the video of me fucking Cole and Hunter, I never heard another word.

As I walked away, they called out for me, saying shit to my back, but I didn't care. I darted across the campus toward the commandant's house to see Sarge. I missed my baby so much it had been hell getting to sleep without her.

Cadets shouted insults at me, telling me it wasn't too late to go home. I raised my hand and gave them the finger. *Assholes.* They could torment me all they wanted. Until I got answers about my father's death, I wasn't going anywhere. Not like I had many options, anyway. My checking account had a few hundred dollars from waiting tables at a bar in Virginia Beach.

Uncle Mark's house was at the center of the massive property. A brick colonial with navy blue shutters and a long covered porch. I balled my hand into a fist, about to knock on his front door, when I heard voices. The door was open a crack, so I pushed on the wood and poked my head inside.

"She's in danger outside of the academy," Mark said. "Until we can find a suitable place for Grace, she's staying here."

A beat passed before another voice said, "And I say she goes."

Cole.

What the fuck was his issue with me?

"I agree with your dad," Hunter interjected. "Keeping Grace here is the smart play. For now, the Founders are happy, and The Lucaya Group can't find her."

Find me?

I stepped inside and quietly closed the door behind me. My heart raced as I leaned against the wall, straining to listen to their conversation. The Founders? The Lucaya Group? I'd never heard Cole mention either of them before. He'd also said something about the Knights during my first dinner at his house when Uncle Mark left in a hurry and never came back to the dining room.

"If Grace's father finds out she's at the academy, he will destroy everything our family has built," Cole said. "There won't be a single brick left of YMA by the time he's done."

You can't trust the people closest to you.

The Marine from my dad's funeral came to mind, his words ringing in my ears. Now I understood what he was trying to tell me. He was warning me about the Marshalls. Mark was my godfather, the one person my dad trusted most. Oliver said the answers were at the academy, and this seemed like a step in the right direction.

Nails tapped on the hardwood floor. Then all conversation ceased. Sarge must have smelled me because she raced down the hallway toward the front door. I pushed off from the wall and held out my arms for her. She jumped up on my thigh, panting like a maniac, begging for me to pet her.

I sank to my knees in front of her and scratched

her behind the ears. "Hey, baby girl." I kissed her head. "Did you miss me?"

She licked my cheek.

"Grace," Mark said as he stepped out from the living room with Cole and Hunter behind him. "I wasn't expecting you."

"Sorry, I missed Sarge so much I had to see her."

"You can't come here during the week," he said in a cold tone. "And you can never come again unannounced."

"Um." I bit my lip, confused by his behavior. "Okay. Is something wrong, Uncle Mark?"

He shoved his hands into the pockets of his navy slacks and sighed. "No, Grace. Everything is fine."

Cole shot dagger eyes at me while Hunter stared at me with fascination. He always had this dopey, lovesick look about him. It was cute, kind of sexy, and also made me wonder what he was thinking.

Much like Cole, Hunter was still somewhat of a mystery to me. They were the type of men who didn't believe in sharing their feelings. God forbid they look weak in front of a woman.

"You can stay for ten minutes," Mark said in a stern tone. "Then, I have to get back to Harper Hall for a meeting."

"On an R&R day?"

"I'm the commandant. I never take a day off."

With that, he spun on his heels, ordering Cole and

Hunter to follow. I sat on the floor and hugged Sarge, kissing her cute face as I watched them disappear into a room at the back of the house.

"What are they up to?" I asked Sarge. "You need to find out for me, girl."

She licked my cheek in response.

If only she understood me.

Grace

I was out of bed before Reveille, midway through fixing my hair in the mirror, when I heard the bugle sound. Anxiety tore through my chest, adrenaline coursing through my body. It was impossible to sit still until Hunter arrived.

He knocked on the door, and I let out a sigh of relief. I flung open the door and smiled at Hunter, who looked drop-dead sexy. He wore navy trousers, the matching blazer with a crisp white shirt, and a gold tie, holding a garrison cap in his hand. As promised, he upheld his end of the bargain and stopped by my room with a freshly pressed uniform.

I took the uniform from his hand and set it on the bed. "Just so we're clear, this is what you owed me from the other day."

"This is the last one until you talk to Cole. I can't get you another one."

"We had a deal, Hunter."

"My hands are tied. I don't have the same connections as Cole. Uniforms are limited. You're lucky a few cadets owed me favors."

"I could just ask my uncle for new uniforms," I pointed out.

Hunter snickered. "But then you would have to tell him what the cadets did. And we both know you're not a snitch, Grace."

"No, but I can't perform sexual favors for the rest of the year just to get basic shit I would have already had if you and Cole hadn't ordered our platoon to fuck up my room."

"They would have done it without Cole giving the order."

"How about you?"

He shook his head. "I was with Cole. But I didn't give my approval."

"No, but you didn't do anything to stop him."

"What do you want from me, Grace? Marshall Law is the only law that matters at this school."

Hunter shut the door and leaned against the wood, his massive body invading every inch of the space. My mind drifted to the night at Cole's house, when Hunter stood in the same position, holding my back against his chest as Cole licked my pussy. They were like starved animals that night. Even though I couldn't stand them now, I still missed them.

He ran a hand through his dark hair, a smirk in place. "C'mon, Grace. Don't you want to have a little fun before you get your ass kicked in cadet training?"

I clenched my teeth as waves of anger pulsed

through me. "Fuck you, Hunter. You pretend to be different, but you're just like Cole. I will finish cadet training and become the first female cadet at YMA. I'm not backing down because someone chased me through the woods."

"Fuck, Grace." He grabbed himself over the front of his pants. "That speech made my cock hard."

"You get hard from a cool breeze." I reached behind him and opened the door. "Get out, Hunter."

He glided his teeth across his lip. "I thought we're friends."

"We *were* friends. Now, we're nothing. I got you off the other day because I needed a favor, not because I want you. Not because I'm the least bit interested in pursuing a relationship with you."

He tilted his head to the side and inspected my face for the lie. "No? We both know that's not true, Grace. You begged for my cock the last time we were together. Just admit you still want me, baby girl. Say it. You want my cock."

"Not anymore. It's time to go. I have to get dressed and ready for inspection before Cole criticizes me in front of our platoon."

A group of cadets strolled past my room, their loud chatter dying down as our eyes met. They stopped and stared like I was the main attraction of the day. I raised my hand and gave them the finger.

Fucking jerks.

The tall blond's nostrils flared. One of them called me a whore, and the other sneered at me. So much for making friends.

Hunter closed the door. "The next time you need a favor, don't come crawling back to me."

"Like you would ever deny me when I'm offering sex."

"I can resist you."

Built like a professional athlete, he was thick in the chest and broad in the shoulders. I'd spent a lot of time over the years worshiping his sexy body, screaming his name, and begging him for more.

I stripped off my shirt and threw it onto the floor. His eyes landed on my bare breasts. My nipples were painfully sore, desperate for him to touch. I blamed it on the cold air in the room, but it was all Hunter. I leaned forward and pulled the dress shirt from his waistband.

"Grace," he said through clenched teeth. "Stop."

"But, Hunter," I said in a sensual tone as I worked on his zipper. "Don't you want this? Don't you want me to put your big cock in my mouth? Hmm..." He was so long and hard that when I unzipped his pants, his dick poked my stomach. "I can make you feel good, Hunter." I stroked him over his black boxer briefs. "So good."

He turned his head, breathing so hard his chest rose and fell. With his arms at his sides, he stood straight and avoided my gaze. It was killing him not to look at me topless. So I took his right hand and placed it over my breast, moving his thumb over my nipple.

"I know you like this, Hunter. Stop denying yourself pleasure."

Torturing him was too much fun. I could use sex as a weapon, wielding it for my deviant purposes.

He drew a breath from between his teeth as his eyes met mine. "Fine, Grace. What do you want?"

Hunter had a lot of connections and could have made my life easier at the academy. But I couldn't forgive him for abandoning me. He was my friend, too, not just Cole's.

"You have no willpower," I remarked with a cocky smirk plastered on my face. "Look how easy it is to distract you."

"Hey," he yelled as I walked away. "Finish what you started, Grace."

"No, I don't think so. You can go now. I have to get dressed."

I lifted the uniform from the bed and ignored Hunter. He could stand over there and pout all he wanted. Until he started treating me like before, I wasn't giving him another hand job, blowjob, nada. He could rub his cock raw for all I cared.

I stepped into the trousers that were a size too big, but they would have to do until I could get new uniforms.

"It's like that," Hunter said with a trace of bitterness to his tone. "Are you going to leave me hanging?" He stood at the center of the room and watched me dress.

"I'm still mad at you. Consider yourself lucky you got a hand job. It's more than what Cole got."

His nose wrinkled with disgust. "You let Cole touch you."

"Because that was about me getting off. There's a difference. He didn't even ask me for sex. He pushed me away when I offered."

Hunter glared at me. "Cole's the one who insisted I stop talking to you. He's the one who pushed you away." He shoved a hand through his hair and sighed. "It wasn't my idea, Grace. I didn't want any of this to happen. We were only trying to keep you safe."

His mouth opened, then slapped shut as if he'd said too much and regretted it. He turned his head to the side and breathed deeply.

"What are you protecting me from?"

"Nothing, Grace. Forget I said anything."

He was at the door in seconds and gone before I could get in another word. I didn't need their protection, nor did I want it. If I was going to become a cadet, I had to do it on my own.

After I checked my appearance in the mirror, I read my schedule one more time.

York Military Academy Schedule

05:30 – Arise for personal fitness workout (optional)
06:30 – Reveille (all hands out of bed)
07:00 – Instruction/Inspection
07:10 – Morning meal formation
07:15 – Morning Meal
07:55 – Calculus III
08:55 – Weapons Systems
09:05 – Advanced Biology
10:00 – Physics II
10:55 – Electrical Engineering
12:00 – Noon meal formation
12:15 – Noon meal
13:00 – Company training time
13:40 – Flight Instruction
14:35 – Aerospace Engineering Capstone
15:50 – Monday through Thursday - Cadet Training
18:15 – Evening meal formation
18:30 – Evening meal
19:30 – Study period
22:00 – Taps for all Cadets

Dressed in the York Military Academy uniform, I stood straight as a board outside of my room. I could hardly breathe as Cole and Hunter walked down the long hallway. The cadets lined up, arms at their sides and heads held high. Hunter was quick and efficient. No bullshit while Cole sized each of us up.

A few of the guys got their asses reamed out by Cole when they let their gazes wander for too long. I had to remember not to look directly at him when he stopped in front of me. Pressing my lips together, I remained expressionless. His careful appraisal of my body set every nerve ending on fire. Just the feel of his eyes roaming over my curves made my insides scorch with desire.

How could I want someone I hated? Why did my traitorous body not get the memo that he was now the bad guy?

Cole spent more time analyzing me than the other cadets as if he were trying to find something wrong with my appearance. I held my breath, my heart beating so fast my head spun. Cole took one last look at me before moving on to the next cadet. The air expelled from my lungs, relief washing over me. I was so sure he would find something about me out of order and punish me for it.

And not the fun kind.

After inspection, we lined up for breakfast and marched toward the mess hall. I sat beside Julian, who was a leftie and kept elbowing me. Cole studied us from the end of the table as if Julian and I were the only people in the room. His eyes practically melted my skin. He'd always watched me like this. Except now, my skin didn't tingle with the same desire. I feared he would never go back to normal and that he would hate me for the rest of his life.

After we ate, I walked with Julian to Prescott Hall, where I had calculus. I wasn't sure what my uncle thought when he signed me up for aerospace engineering. I hated math. At my last college, I majored in computer science. I guess he thought that meant I could be an engineer, though the majors were nothing alike.

Cole, Hunter, and Brax shuffled into Weapons Systems class attached at the hip. They never seemed to go anywhere without the other. Like me, Cole majored in aerospace engineering. Hunter wanted to be a nuclear engineer. Brax was a few credits shy of a degree in electrical engineering.

Despite their dirty mouths, Cole and Hunter were brilliant. Their families had spent a lot of money ensuring they would have lucrative careers. And given the nature of their family's businesses, they needed advanced degrees. Throughout each period, I could sense them watching me. Just knowing they were in the same room made my skin flush.

We had company training time after lunch. Cole and Hunter worked our asses hard for those thirty minutes, and by the time we finished, it relieved me to discover I had one class without one of them. At least flight instruction was a class I could pass with flying colors.

As I walked into the aviation classroom, my mouth fell open in shock. The man from my father's funeral, the Marine who had insisted I come to York Military Academy for answers, stood beside the wooden desk at the front of the room.

Oliver.

My gaze drifted to the insignia on his epaulettes. He was a captain in the Marine Corps but looked too young to have climbed the ranks that fast. This wasn't a real military school affiliated with a particular branch of service. So why would an active Marine be my new flight instructor?

His eyes hadn't left mine from the moment I entered the room. Oliver acknowledged me with a quick nod. I took a seat toward the middle of the classroom, attempting to blend in with the others. The rest of the boys shuffled into their places, filling out the surrounding seats.

Oliver turned his back to the class to write a few things on the chalkboard. "I'm Captain Fox. I will be your flight instructor until the end of the semester."

A boy raised his hand. "Will we get to fly a plane?"

Oliver nodded. "At some point, yes. But first, you need to learn the basics, starting with aircraft category and aircraft classification. Who read the first five chapters of the textbook?"

Every hand flew in the air.

"Aircraft category refers to the certification of the aircraft based on the intended use or operating limitations. There are four main types of aircraft classification—normal, utility, primary, and acrobatic."

Since I was way beyond the basics and already had my pilot's license, I focused on Oliver's delicious mouth, staring at his lips with each word he spoke. The cadets took notes, typing feverishly on their notebook computers. I didn't even own a computer. Wherever we moved, I used the free ones on base to do my homework.

"Let's say your FAA license says you can fly an airplane that's single or multi-engine land," Oliver said. "Can I fly any airplane?"

The room fell silent as he waited for an answer.

I raised my hand.

"Hale?"

"No, sir. You have to satisfy other requirements."

"Very good." He grinned. "Does anyone know what type of license I would need to fly an airplane that weighs over twelve thousand five hundred pounds? What about a jet that has a turbo-powered engine?"

My hand shot in the air.

"Brown noser," someone behind me groaned.

Oliver pointed at me.

"You would need a type rating, sir."

"Good job, Hale. A type rating shows which group

of airplanes you can fly." Oliver gave me an approving grin. Then his eyes swept over the room. "For those of you who are unaware, Hale's father was one of the best pilots in Marine Corps history."

"Couldn't have been that good," someone whispered.

Another boy laughed. "He died in a helicopter crash he caused."

Oliver's face twisted with anger. "Who said that?"

No one raised their hand.

I felt as if the room had slipped out from under me. "Don't you dare talk about my dad."

"What are you going to do about it, GI Barbie?" Preston taunted.

Oliver moved to the front of his desk, his jaw set hard. "Speak now, or I'm writing all of you up. If someone doesn't come forward by the end of the class, I'm docking fifty points from First Platoon."

"That's not fair," someone shouted. "We did nothing wrong."

"Come forward," Oliver demanded. "Whoever said that owes Hale an apology."

"Sorry," a guy groaned.

"Did you say it?" Oliver asked him.

He shook his head. "No, sir. But I'm not losing points."

Oliver looked as if he were trying to keep his cool. "Colonel John Hale was a decorated war hero," he told the class, and my heart swelled with pride, thankful for his kind words. "He saved my life. That was the last thing he did before he took his final breath." His eyes roamed over the room, then moved to me. "If it weren't for his bravery and skill, I wouldn't be here right now."

"Do it." A cadet smacked his friend on the arm.

"No," the blond with a buzz-cut mumbled.

"Both of you," Captain Fox boomed, his eyes on the boys. "Come to my office after class. You can start serving your punishment then."

"But I didn't say it."

His friend snickered.

"Asshole."

Captain Fox strolled down the center of the aisle. The cadet's eyes lowered to the desk.

"I think that answers the question." He looked at the culprits with fire in his eyes. "I'll be speaking with your platoon commander." Folding his arms over his chest, he glared at them. "And if you speak out of turn in my classroom again, I'll see to your removal from the academy."

"You can't do that," the cadet shot back. "My father is one of the primary donors. The board would never let that happen."

Captain Fox's jaw ticked. "Do it again and find out."

Then he turned his back on the boys and resumed

his place in front of the chalkboard. His eyes flicked to mine for a second, and I mouthed *thank you*. I didn't have many allies at this school and could use as many as I could get. Sure, he was a professor and off-limits. But there weren't any rules about being friendly with him.

After class ended, Oliver leaned back against the blackboard, studying me with curiosity. His lips parted like he wanted to say something. So I walked down the aisle and stopped in front of his desk.

I waved awkwardly. "You look too young to be a captain."

He smirked. "I'm older than I look. How are you adjusting to YMA?"

"I'm not exactly welcome here."

"You're Commandant Marshall's test case. He's been wanting to make YMA co-ed for years and keeps getting turned down by the board."

Which leaves no room for failure...

"This is just a private school full of rich kids."

He chuckled. "You're not wrong about that, but YMA is a good school. A lot of officers and politicians went here. It will look good on your resume if you want to follow in your dad's footsteps."

I shook my head. "No, I'm not a risk my life for my country kind of girl. And after what happened to my dad..."

He clutched my shoulder to comfort me. "Look,

Grace, I'm sure this is hard for you. It's only been a week since the funeral. If anyone bothers you, let me know, okay? I'll take care of them."

Tension crackled in the air between us. When I looked up and into his eyes, my heart slammed into my ribcage. He was gorgeous, tall, and muscular, filling out every inch of his uniform perfectly. I glanced at his hand on my shoulder, which he removed in an instant, and stepped back a few feet to create an ocean between us.

"You said to come here for answers. Can you give them to me?"

"Yes, but outside of this classroom. We have to be careful." He cleared his throat and lowered his voice. "There's a place where we can meet. If you follow the path to Kingston Field, make a right and go straight toward the beach. There's a walking trail in the woods right before you reach the beach. Take the fork in the path and follow it to the boulder until you see an abandoned church."

"The cadets know about the chapel. It's not a secret."

"They will be in bed when we meet." He lowered his voice. "Your father's death wasn't an accident."

My jaw unhinged from his confession. "Are you sure?"

"I was there, Grace."

I didn't know him. What if he was telling me all

this to lure me to the creepy church and kill me? If someone had murdered my dad, then I could be a loose end. I knew nothing about my dad's work. Just that he was a pilot and often had to leave for unplanned missions with almost no notice. As a kid, I thought nothing of it. But as an adult, I wondered if the military sanctioned all of his trips.

I grabbed his jacket, holding his gaze. "Tell me what happened."

"On Sunday night, meet me at the chapel at 2300 hours."

Six days from now.

He cleared his throat and looked away. "You should go."

I dropped my hand, now feeling somewhat stupid for getting over emotional, and rushed out of the room as if it was on fire.

Grace

S weat slid down my forehead, dripping from every place imaginable as I raced through the obstacle course. Cadet training was like boot camp on steroids.

We started our trek on the opposite side of campus. A few of the cadets tried to trip me before the staff yelled for them to focus on themselves. Thankfully, I lost a bunch of them when we ran across the soccer field and into the woods.

A shiver rolled down my arms at the thought of the last time I was here. Someone had chased me, made me think I was losing my mind. Until Cole and the others had shown up, I thought someone was trying to kill me.

Would the cadets go that far to get rid of me?

I pushed down the fear and anxiety. My dad had forced me to endure survival training each year before living with the Marshalls for the summer. He had insisted I learn how to fend off attackers, though I never understood why.

When had I ever been in danger?

I followed the red arrows painted on the trees until

I spotted a wooden wall with ropes dangling from it. One cadet pulled himself to the top, taking one last look at me before he dropped to the other side.

I thought our first day of cadet training would be simple shit like pushups or running a few laps on the beach. Nope, they forced us to run the entire obstacle course we had to pass to become a cadet after the eight weeks. To see if we were even cut out to be at the academy.

I grabbed a rope, which burned my sweaty palms, and climbed the wall. A thick canopy overhead blocked the sun from view, providing some shade, and I was thankful for that. The sun had beaten down on my face, pounding on my back as I ran through the first part of the course.

The cadet beside me reached over and tried to shake me off the rope. I swung from side to side, my cheek smacking into the wooden wall.

"Asshole," I gritted out. "Stop cheating."

"You don't belong here," he shot back.

I pushed off from the wall and put some distance between us. He kicked me with his boot and hit the back of my thigh. I lost my grip, sliding down the rope, and my palms rubbed raw as I dropped toward the ground.

Don't look down, I reminded myself. *Never look down.*

I tightened my grip on the rope, swinging at an awkward angle. The brown-haired cadet smirked as he disappeared over the wall. *Good riddance*, I thought, though my relief came too soon. Because within seconds, another cadet scaled the wall. He didn't waste a second, coming for me with a plan. Most of the cadets in my training class were freshmen. I wasn't their competition. We didn't share any classes or meals.

So why the hell were they attacking me?

I reached the top of the wall with a few more pulls on the rope, desperate to get away from the cadets before I ended up with a cracked skull. Once my feet hit the ground on the other side, I took off down the path. Staff members dressed in uniform studied me with stopwatches in their hands, clicking buttons as I passed.

The soles of my boots pounded the dirt, my legs tingling with exhaustion. When I hit the beach, I let out a sigh of relief. Following the rest of the pack, I ran toward the final course and dropped to my knees in front of the line in the sand. Flattening onto my stomach, I inched beneath the black mesh.

Every bone and muscle in my body ached. My arms and legs were so close to failing me. But with all the adrenaline coursing through my veins, it gave me the second wind I needed.

Someone yanked on my boot, pulling me toward them. "Get the fuck out of the way, Hale."

"Get off me!" I kicked him, hoping my boot hit his face.

He groaned. "Fucking bitch."

Ignoring him, I kept going, allowing the other cadets hatred for me to help me reach the finish line. I hopped to my feet, now in the middle of the pack, as I bolted down the beach toward the last leg of the challenge.

A dozen cadets climbed up the vertical cargo net attached to two wooden posts. My upper body wasn't as strong as before my father's deployment. He always kept me in line, pushed me harder. Dad never took a day off, his mental and physical health his top priorities.

I needed to train to gain an advantage over the cadets who had more experience than me. Cadets like Cole and Hunter would eat me alive in an obstacle course of this magnitude. I was even willing to bet they probably held the fastest completion times.

Using the last of my energy, I grabbed the cargo net. My hands bled from the rope challenge. Sand and sweat slid into the tiny cuts, which hurt like fucking hell. I wanted to give up. So badly, I wished I could walk away and never look back.

But my dad would have been proud of me.

He would have cheered me on.

The staff carefully watched us in our final seconds, making it impossible for the cadet trainees to mess with me. When I reached the top, I looked down for a split second, not the least bit surprised to find Cole with his hands on his hips. I wasn't sure what I expected of him. My friend would have been proud of me for beating half of the cadets on the first try.

But not this version of Cole.

He glared at me with the hatred of a thousand lifetimes. His cold blue eyes sliced right through me as I ran across the finish line in the sand.

An officer hit a button on his stopwatch and said, "Not bad for the first try, Hale." He showed me the watch. Five minutes and thirty-two seconds. "You have a long way to go. By the end of the training, you better be under four minutes."

"Yes, sir."

Cole shot me a nasty look, with his arms crossed over his muscular chest. His uniform molded to his arms and thighs. And for a moment, I thought about what hid beneath his clothes.

Stop it, Grace.

I could not let him distract me. Cole was my weakness, but he was also my strength. For years, he'd been my everything. So it sucked not having him on my side.

Without another thought, I turned away from Cole and headed toward the water cooler. I wouldn't let him take this small victory from me.

ON MY WAY back to the barracks, I ran into Braxton Cade. He crossed the courtyard when he spotted me dragging ass after the most demanding workout of my life. Every muscle and bone in my body ached. Sweat matted my hair, my ponytail clinging to my neck. Brax gave me a quick once over, and surprisingly, he didn't look disgusted by my wet dog appearance.

"I heard you made it through the obstacle course on the first try." He grinned. "Did Cole tell you that most of the male cadets don't make it more than halfway?"

I peeked up at him and all of his tattooed sexiness. "No, I didn't know that. How about you? Did you make it?"

"I was one of the worst in my cadet class." He tipped his head back and laughed. "I couldn't even pass the rope challenge. You should have seen me trying to climb that damn thing. I looked like such a pathetic asshole."

I laughed. "And look at you now." My eyes might have traveled up and down the length of his toned body once or twice. Maybe three times. "I bet you can run the course in under two minutes now."

"It only took me four years to get in good enough shape to do it."

"What about Cole and Hunter?"

He snickered. "Those dickheads smoked the

185

competition. They never let me forget it. Cole still holds the record."

"Oh, yeah? How fast can he run it?"

"One minute twenty-three seconds."

My mouth dropped in shock. "Are you shitting me?"

"Nope." Brax shook his head. "I've seen him do it more than once."

"Damn. That's insane. I would have come in sooner if the cadets hadn't tried to kill me a few times along the way."

"Excuses," he quipped with a cheeky grin.

"If it weren't for those jerks, I would have been closer to four minutes."

"I won't lie to you, Grace. Everyone here wants to see you fail. They want you to leave. No one at YMA likes change."

"You would think some cadets wouldn't mind having a girl around."

"Oh, they want to fuck you," he clarified. "Any sane man would."

My cheeks flushed at his compliment.

"But don't get it twisted, girl. They are out for blood. We take the War Games seriously. And since it's our last year, no one wants to lose the bragging rights."

"What difference does it make who wins? You'll leave at the end of the year and forget all about this place. It's just a silly game."

"You're new here." He dipped his head down and lowered his voice. "So let me give you some advice. The War Games are sacred. It's an honor to win the Command Cup."

Brax's closeness garnered attention from onlookers who passed us on our way to the dormitory. It also made my body all too aware of his masculine scent, a mixture of spicy soap and laundry detergent. He plucked a pack of gum from the inside pocket of his blazer and offered a piece to me. I took a stick as he folded the gum onto his tongue.

"No talking shit about the War Games." I nodded. "Got it. Anything else I should know?"

"It's best you stay off everyone's radar as much as possible. Don't attract attention to yourself."

I snickered at his bold remark. "I won't downplay my achievements to make these jerks feel better about themselves."

Brax rolled his big shoulders, his eyes on the cadets passing us, who shot daggers at me. "Some cadets would kill you to get rid of you."

"They hate me that much? What the fuck is wrong with these spoiled brats?"

"Nah. It's not personal. They hate the *idea* of you at their school. Not you as a person." He laughed as if enjoying a private joke. "But you got the spoiled part right. This isn't like a normal boarding school or a real military academy. We live by a certain code, one many of us have followed for years. Your admission fucked up the status quo around here. Some people think it's time to remove the Marshalls from power, which has been causing a lot of problems for Cole."

I waved off his comment with my hand. "Please, Cole runs this school. He makes the rules."

"The donors and their sons want to see the Marshalls dethroned because of you."

Guilt ripped through my chest, though I wasn't sure why I felt anything at all. My uncle had insisted I come to York Military Academy for the year.

"How do you feel about me being here?"

"Doesn't matter to me," he said with a shrug. "You're not like other girls."

I groaned at his comment. "Seriously? I hate when guys say that."

"Well, you're not." Brax laughed as he looked over at me. "Few women could make it through an obstacle course designed by a Navy SEAL on the first try. Each year, YMA sends over thirty percent of the cadet class home before the end of the fall semester. A lot of the incoming plebes train before they come here. So when a girl breezes through the course, you're going to have a lot of pissed-off cadets."

"I didn't breeze through it. That was hard fucking work."

"The Colonel trained you well."

A smile touched my lips. "He did."

"Cole and Hunter's parents bred them for the academy," Brax added. "But not me. My dad only sent me to YMA because he thought this place would turn me into a man and make me more responsible. My dad is an asshole. Nothing is ever good enough for him."

"My dad was tough, too."

We passed a group of cadets who tipped their heads at Brax, then shot me a nasty look. By now, everyone had probably heard the news about my first run at the obstacle course. Despite a few setbacks, I was proud of myself for completing it.

"We have something in common," Brax commented. "At least in your case, having a dad who was hard on you benefited you."

"You turned out okay."

Brax was always nice to me when I hung out with him at Cole's house. But I had to keep reminding myself that I could not trust Cole and his friends.

At Bryant Hall, he opened the door for me. I waited for a few cadets to pass through before I stepped inside the building, headed toward the stair-well. My room was on the second floor at the far end of the hall. I was curious about where Cole, Hunter, and Brax lived, so I let him lead the way.

We climbed the stairs to the second deck, and midway down the corridor, Brax halted at Room 207. "This is my stop." He tipped his head at the door. "Wanna come in? We have contraband alcohol."

I tugged on my sweaty shirt and shook my head. "Thanks for the offer, but no. I have to shower. And with how tense things are between Cole and me, I think it's best I keep my distance."

Brax leaned his shoulder against the wall. "If you change your mind, you know where to find me."

"Thanks, Brax."

He winked, then headed into the apartment he shared with *my* cadets.

Grace

B y the end of the week, the two uniforms Hunter borrowed for me smelled like sweat. They were also wrinkled beyond repair.

That morning, Cole yelled at me in front of our platoon and clarified that I better look presentable for our next inspection. My cheeks flamed as he bent down and took a whiff.

It wasn't my fault.

I'd taken a shower every night before bed and tried to keep my uniforms clean. But I needed a washing machine and an iron and didn't have either of those things.

The cadets sent their clothes to a cleaning service. But I couldn't afford that luxury. There was a laundry room in the basement of Bryant Hall, but I didn't have any detergent. I could wash my uniform in the sink water that smelled like rotten eggs or beg Cole for new uniforms.

Thanks to Brax walking me home from my first cadet training, I knew where the assholes lived. So I sucked up my pride and walked down the hall to room 207.

Hunter opened the door after I knocked a second time. He stood in the entry, shirtless and only wearing a pair of super-tight black boxer briefs. *Fuck me.* I could barely look at him without blushing… or thinking about how much I still wanted him.

The corners of Hunter's mouth tipped up into a wicked grin. "What are you doing here, baby girl?"

"Is Cole here?"

"He's not in a good mood," he said in a hushed tone. "Come back later."

"No, I have to talk to him about getting new uniforms."

"He's not in a charitable mood, Grace. Trust me. Come back later."

Ignoring his suggestion, I pushed on the door and stepped into the living room. It was an open concept apartment with the living room and kitchen in one room and bedrooms on each side of the space.

Two of the doors were open, and a half-naked Brax leaned against the wall outside one of them. He held a tablet in front of him, drawing on it with the digital pen in his hand as he looked at me. Brax was into graphic design and never without a drawing tablet in his hand.

"Did you come to drink with us?" Brax asked me.

"No, I came to beg for new uniforms."

"Oh, I like the sound of this." Brax pushed off the wall, setting his tablet on the kitchen island before he walked into the living room. He stopped a few feet from me, his eyes traveling up and down my body with desire. "Hey, Cole. Come out here."

"Fuck off," Cole yelled through his closed door.

His room was at the back of the apartment, on the right side of the kitchen.

Brax cupped his hands around his mouth and yelled, "Grace is here."

With that, two doors swung open. Cole emerged from the back of the apartment with his blond hair unusually messy as if he had been pulling it. Then Julian approached from the left side of the apartment, exiting the first room off the living room.

"Hey, girl," Julian said with a smile. "What are you doing here?"

"I don't recall inviting you," Cole snapped before I could respond. "Who said you could stop by the officer's living quarters after hours?"

"What is wrong with you, Cole?" I rushed over to him and smacked his hard chest. "I can't stand this shit anymore."

He clutched my wrist with a heated look in his eyes. "You need to leave, Grace. Now."

"No, not until you give me new uniforms."

"Just give her the fucking uniforms," Julian shouted.

Cole cocked his head at him with a crazed look in his eyes. "Stay the fuck out of this, Archer. Go back to your fucking room and shut your fucking mouth."

"No." Julian crossed the room and got in Cole's face. "Every cadet gets five uniforms provided by the academy."

"Grace has five uniforms."

Julian balled his hands into a fists. "Not ones she can wear, asshole."

Cole's nostrils flared, and before I could get out of the way, I was in the middle of a fight between the two cadet colonels. I ducked down as Julian threw the first punch. He was so sweet and always defending my honor. I saw myself with someone like Julian, but I feared I would never let Cole go.

My heart, mind, and body wanted Cole.

Even if he didn't love me back.

Brax grabbed my arm and pulled me out of the way. "You picked a bad night to show up, *chica.*"

"What happened?"

"Cole got into another fight with the commandant."

Hunter ripped Julian and Cole apart, ordering them to different sides of the living room as I stood beside Brax. He was the safe one in the group. At least he seemed like the safe bet. It was always the quiet ones that surprised me, though, so I had to remember that when I felt my walls coming down around him.

"That's enough," Hunter yelled with his arms pushed out at his sides to maintain a distance between the other cadets. "You two are always at each other's throats. Learn to live with each other before I kick both of your asses."

The three of them argued back and forth, their voices so loud I wondered if people in the hallway could hear them. So I used this time to see if I could get some information out of Brax. He was the nicest of the bunch and the most forthcoming.

"How do you feel about Julian living here?" I asked Brax in a hushed tone.

He shrugged. "He seems okay, I guess. I don't know. There's something about him I don't like. I can't put my finger on it."

"Do you think Cole is right about him?"

"Only time will tell. So far, he hasn't done anything to raise any suspicions."

"I like him."

"I know."

I peeked up at Brax. "That's why Cole hates him."

He bobbed his head in agreement.

After the drama in the room settled down, all eyes landed on me. Hunter gave me his usual sexy grin that made me want to climb his muscular body and have my way with him. Julian tugged at the collar of his YMA Athletics T-shirt and bit his lip.

I moved toward him. "You didn't have to do that for me."

Hunter yanked me away from Julian, pressing my back against his chest. "Stay away from him, baby girl."

"She's not your baby girl," Julian said.

"Grace is whatever the fuck I say she is."

"No more fighting. I appreciate you getting involved, Julian, but it's not worth spending the rest of the year with all the cadets attacking you."

"You're worth it," he said without hesitation. "If they're too stupid to see that, then fuck them."

Cole scrubbed a hand across his perfectly shaven jaw and studied me. He wasn't the same boy who'd welcomed me into his home and held my hand while we watched Captain America. I so desperately wanted him to be that boy again, even if it was only for a moment.

"I don't want any trouble," I said to Cole. "I just want my uniforms. Okay?"

A smirk turned up the right corner of his delicious mouth. "How do you plan to wash them?"

"I'll figure it out."

"I can help with that," Julian offered.

Thank you, I mouthed, and he smiled.

"Don't go making eyes at our girl," Cole said to Julian, then his gaze moved to me. "And don't you dare accept charity from this sick motherfucker, or you will regret it."

I pushed my hands onto my hips. "Is that so?"

"Yeah, that's so, Grace." He hovered over me, breathing minty toothpaste in my face. "Do you remember what I said the night of the bonfire?"

"About Julian being a murdering liar? Yeah, how could I forget that."

"What?" Julian stammered. "Why are you telling Grace I killed someone?"

"Because you did," Cole fired back. "Blackwell Military Academy might not have found evidence of your wrongdoing, but I know you killed your roommate. And I intend to prove it."

"Go ahead," Julian challenged. "Because you'll find out I didn't touch him. I wasn't even on the same side of the campus at the time of his death. The school and the police have video footage and reports from the medical examiner that prove my innocence."

"Please. You could have faked that shit, which leaves your word against a dead guy. And since he's not talking, I'll find other ways to prove you killed him."

"I didn't touch him," Julian said in a stern tone.

"Okay, that's enough of the blame game," I said to steer the conversation in another direction. "I need three more uniforms, some laundry detergent, and an iron."

"No," Cole said in a dismissive tone before he

walked across the room and plopped down on the sectional couch.

I marched over to him, standing in front of the coffee table to keep some distance from him. "Here's the deal, Cole. You can give me new uniforms and supplies, or I'm going to let Preston, Rhys, and Grayson fuck me until I get what I want. It's your choice. And this time, I'll send the video to you, so you can watch."

His jaw ticked. "You wouldn't fuck them. I'm calling your bluff."

"Rhys has wanted to fuck me for years. So has Grayson. They want what they think you have, except they are too stupid to realize you lost me a long time ago." I cracked my knuckles. "What's it gonna be, Cole?"

As I angled my body to walk away, Cole said, "Wait."

I turned to face him, and his lips parted with a mixture of desire and hatred. "You don't have the guts to do it."

"Watch me."

I strolled toward the door, expecting Cole to stop me, but it was Hunter who said, "Grace, don't." Then he said to Cole, "What the fuck is your problem, Marshall? She's our girl. I'm not letting those bastards put their mark on her."

"I second that," Brax said. "Grace is better off with us."

"Fine," Cole grunted. "You want uniforms, brat? Then work for them."

"What do I have to do?"

Cole leaned forward on the couch, a smirk pulling at his features. "Strip."

"Excuse me?"

"You heard me, little brat. Take off your clothes."

"No," Julian said from behind me. "Don't do anything he says."

Cole pointed his finger at Julian. "Go to your room, Archer. This doesn't involve you."

"Grace, you don't have to do this," Julian insisted. "Please."

I folded my arms over my chest, and Cole's eyes landed on my breasts. The fabric covered them, but he stared as if my cleavage were popping out of the top.

"You're down to your last pair of clean PT sweats," he said. "If you want to get them dirty, that's your choice."

My eyebrows rose in confusion. "What are you talking about?"

"Clean our apartment," he said with zero emotion in his tone.

"No way. You're out of your mind."

"How bad do you want new uniforms, Grace? If you fail another inspection, you'll lose points for our

199

platoon. And if that were to happen, you would jeopardize our standing for the War Games. Now you don't want that, do you? Because you're smart enough to understand the cadets will kill to win the Games. So strip or not. That's your choice. Better get cleaning before I change my mind."

Anger surged through my veins. I expelled the air from my lungs, trying to keep my cool as I stared him down. The bastard was serious. He wanted me to earn my uniforms. *Dickhead.* Well, to hell with him. Cole would not win this game. Nope, I had a plan that would make him regret suggesting this silly idea.

I moved between Cole's spread thighs and inched my shirt up my stomach. His lips parted, his chest rising and falling as I dragged my shirt over my head.

"Grace," Julian warned. "Don't do it."

"It's okay," I assured him. "I can handle him."

Cole had seen me naked hundreds of times. We had no boundaries with our bodies. I dropped my shirt onto Cole's lap, and he clenched his jaw as if he were trying to control himself. His cold, blue eyes landed on my tits that were stuffed into a black sports bra. He laid his head back on the cushion and watched as I shoved the sweatpants down my hips.

Thankfully, I was wearing boy shorts instead of a thong, so it was the same as cleaning in a bathing suit. If Cole thought this would embarrass me, he would have to try harder. I owned skimpier bikinis.

"This is a punishment for us," Hunter hissed. "Just give Grace the uniforms before all of us have blue balls for the rest of the night."

Cole turned his head to the side and looked at Hunter, who was now standing on my right. "Unlike you, I can control myself."

Hunter laughed. "Not with Grace."

I took off my shoes and stepped out of the sweatpants, fully aware I had four sets of eyes on my tits and ass. It was exciting yet terrifying to have so many men see me in such a vulnerable position. The cotton sports bra and boy shorts molded to my body and were a size too small.

I bent forward, placing my hands on Cole's thighs as I met his gaze and licked my lips. "Where do you want me to start, sir?"

"Jesus," Hunter groaned.

Brax echoed the same sentiment, while Julian didn't speak a word. He couldn't stop me from following through with the plan.

"The kitchen," Cole bit out.

I tipped my head at his hard cock, which looked as if it were about to poke through his pants. "Hunter is right, Cole. You're only punishing yourself." Just to be a real brat, I grabbed him over top of his sweats, giving him a quick stroke, before I headed into the kitchen.

Cole groaned as I walked away.

"You're an asshole," Hunter muttered.

"Enough," Cole said to end the conversation.

I searched under the kitchen sink for a bucket and cleaning supplies. All four of them stared at me as I added Mr. Clean to the bucket and filled it with water. A lemon scent floated through the air. It was nice to turn on the water and not have it smell like rotten eggs.

To make sure Cole had the worst blue balls of his life, I took the bucket and a rag and moved to the other side of the marble island. I climbed up on a barstool and leaned forward, sticking my butt in the air as I reached across the counter to wipe it down.

Hunter grunted as if he were in physical pain. Even Brax made a guttural sound. Cole and Julian were quiet, and I wasn't sure what to make of all the silence. Knowing Cole, he was on the couch stewing while Julian was upset with my decision.

He couldn't come to my rescue every time.

After I finished cleaning the counter, I hopped down from the stool. All of them stared at me with their boners aimed in my direction. The head of Hunter's big cock poked through the slit in his boxer briefs. Julian reached into his sweats to fix himself, and Brax didn't even bother to hide his attraction to me.

I wondered what it would be like to have all four of them. I hated myself for the sick thought. But was it really that sick? I'd already been with Cole and Hunter at the same time.

"Get back to cleaning," Cole ordered when I stood there for a second too long. "You don't have all night."

"Yes, sir," I said in a seductive tone.

I turned my back to them, wiped down the counter next to the stove, and straightened the jars of protein powder. For guys, they were pretty clean. Cole liked order, and so did Hunter. Brax I wasn't sure about, and Julian seemed to thrive in chaos. But he'd grown up attending boarding schools and military academies, so I assumed he was also a neat freak.

Footsteps pounded the tiled floor behind me. And then Hunter's manly scent filled my nostrils as he hooked his arm around my middle. His big hand slid down my stomach, and he dipped his head into the crook of my neck, his breath fanning across my skin. I felt all of him pressed into my backside, which ripped an unintentional moan from my lips.

"Fuck, baby girl," he whispered in my ear. "I can't take it."

"Let her finish," Cole shouted from the living room.

"Nah," Hunter countered. "She's done cleaning our apartment." He nuzzled my neck. "Isn't that right, baby? Come help me with something in my bedroom."

My skin flushed from his words, igniting a fire deep inside me. I clutched his wrist and encouraged him to dip his hand into my panties. Cole had a rule with me, one Hunter had never broken before. But I could tell he was close to giving in to his desires.

"Touch me, Hunter," I begged in a sultry tone to entice him. "Don't listen to Cole."

"Hunter," Cole yelled.

Hunter ignored Cole and slid his hand down with only a second of deliberation, stealing a whimper from my mouth. His finger glided up and down my wet slit, stroking me. I gripped the edge of the counter for support and closed my eyes.

"Oh, my God, Hunter," I whispered.

Cole must have shot to his feet because it sounded like he flipped the coffee table. A loud rustle ensued behind us, and then Hunter's hand slipped out of my underwear. He staggered backward and crashed into the island, replaced by an angry Cole.

"What the fuck, Marshall," Hunter growled.

He only called Cole by his last name when he was mad.

Cole's eyes widened as he sucked in a deep breath and studied me with his thick arms crossed. "Did I say you can touch him?"

"Technically, Hunter touched me."

"The correct answer is no."

I took a step backward, and Cole inched forward, the heat from his body making my skin feel as if it were on fire. Since Cole wouldn't back down, I decided I would play along.

I hopped onto the counter and spread my thighs for him. "Let me guess. You want the same deal I had with Hunter?"

He shot Hunter an irritated look. "What deal was that?"

"A favor for a favor."

Cole shook his head. "I don't want sex for favors." His lips brushed mine, his breath warming my skin. "I want you on your knees scrubbing my floor."

"Liar." I ran my hands up my thighs to tease him. "Just admit it, Cole. You want to fuck me."

"Next room." Cole pointed at the bathroom. "Go. You have one more hour before Taps. If you're not done by then, you're going back to your room without uniforms."

I loved it when Cole went into full-blown drill sergeant mode. It was so fucking hot I wished he would take his head out of his ass and bend me over the island. But he seemed content with making me feel like shit, a recurring theme with Cole.

"I need a mop."

He walked away without another word. Then Hunter moved into his place, looking like a sexy military god with his muscled chest on display and his hard cock tenting his black boxer briefs. I ran my fingers over his skin, tracing my way down to the waistband of his boxers.

"Are you done playing Cole's game?"

Hunter glanced over at Cole, who retrieved a mop from the closet and then found my gaze once more. "You know I want you, Grace. That was never the issue."

"Then what's the issue? Because I don't understand what is going on with either of you."

Cole curled my fingers around the mop. "Get to work, Cinderella. You don't have until the stroke of midnight."

Grace

O n Sunday night, right before 2300 hours, I stepped out of my room dressed in a black hoodie and sweatpants. I slipped the hood over my head and crept down the hallway, holding my breath as I inched toward the stairwell.

Nerves crawled down my arms like spiders. This was probably a terrible idea. No, this was the worst idea of my life. I was sneaking out to meet a professor after hours.

How ridiculous?

I made it to the first floor before I heard voices floating down the corridor. Pressing my back to the wall, I let my arms hang at my sides. My heart raced, the blood pumping through my veins at an impressive rate.

"We need to get rid of her," someone said. "She's going to fuck up everything we've worked for the past three years."

A man grunted in agreement. "Our platoon is winning the War Games this year. I won't let her get in the way."

207

What was the big deal with the War Games? Even Brax had mentioned it on our walk back to the barracks. You would have thought they were competing in the damn Olympics.

Then another voice said, "Marshall said she's fair game."

"Banks doesn't want her either."

Pain ripped through my chest. I clutched my side for comfort, bending forward to suck in a deep breath. Had years of friendship with Cole and Hunter meant nothing to them? I thought they would eventually realize they were acting like jerks and stop making my life hell.

My sweaty palm slid down the wall, and I tripped, my boots squeaking across the tiled floor.

"Did you hear that?"

I stood painfully still, barely breathing, hiding behind a stone column.

Please don't come down here.

A moment of silence passed.

"Tomorrow," one man said in a hushed tone.

Their conversation turned to whispers, then ceased as three sets of shoes slapped the tiled floor, headed in the opposite direction.

That was a close call.

I left Bryant Hall with my hood up and my head low. The wind whipped through the dark, desolate campus. With the beach only a tenth of a mile from the school, I heard waves crashing from a distance. I hurried down Walker Pass, which cut through the center of the campus, leading me to the tennis court at the edge of the property.

When I reached the woods, I glanced over my shoulder. Anxiety pricked my skin, creating tiny bumps down my arms, the anticipation killing me. Swatting at the underbrush, I took the path toward the beach and followed the marked trees as a guide.

For at least ten minutes, I wandered down the trails, my skin crawling with each hoot and howl until I found the old chapel. The structure looked as if a hurricane hit it, the stained glass windows thick with grime. Even the angels on them looked as if they were screaming for help. A massive tree had fallen on the chapel, collapsing the roof. I wondered how the place was still standing. It must have been by the grace of God because there was no logical reason it hadn't crumbled to the ground.

Captain Fox stood on the dilapidated porch and leaned his back against the wall, his thick arms crossed over his chest. My flight instructor wore dark jeans and a short-sleeved black shirt tight against his chest and biceps.

"Thanks for meeting me," I muttered.

Captain Fox stepped forward, now only a few feet from me, the scent of citrus wafting off his skin. He raised his hand and beckoned me with his index finger.

"Come inside. Someone could be watching you. There are eyes and ears everywhere on campus."

Most of the interior of the church was still intact. The tree had fallen on the right side of the building, and the moonlight peeking through provided some of the light.

"Was this used by the academy at one time?" I asked him.

He nodded. "Until the late eighties."

I inched my way down the aisle set between the pews. "What happened to it?"

"A Nor'easter tore apart the coast. After they cleared the debris, the board of directors decided not to restore the chapel."

"It's kind of creepy hiding a church in the middle of the woods."

"The church was here before the school."

He pointed at the front pew. "You should sit for what I have to tell you."

Fear slid down my spine. "Is it that bad?"

"It's not good."

He stood with his hands shoved into his pockets, which only highlighted the muscles in his arms. I dropped to the wooden bench in front of him. Then he hunched down in front of me, cupping his knees with his palms.

"Your dad was a good man, a good Marine. I trusted him with my life." His eyes lowered for a moment to the dirt-covered floor, then slowly found mine. "I was on the chopper with your dad when someone shot it down."

Tears blurred my vision. "How did you survive?"

"Your dad maintained control long enough to steer us over the water. He told me to jump. I didn't want to leave him behind, but he insisted. He said I had to live because I had to find you."

"What were his last words?"

"Tell Gracie I love her."

Before I could stop them from falling, tears streamed down my cheeks. I leaned forward, clutching my stomach as I sobbed. "Did he say anything else?"

Oliver lifted a wooden box from the pew and set it on my lap. It had a dragon symbol carved into the wood. I'd never seen it before, confused why my father would have left this for me.

He handed me a small envelope. "Your dad told me where to find this."

"I'm not ready," I sobbed. "I can't open it..."

"You want answers." Oliver placed his hand over mine on my knee. "I'm not sure what's inside. But it might offer you some closure. Whatever your dad wanted to tell you may help you find peace."

I cried in front of my professor.

At least the cadets weren't around.

I squeezed his hand for comfort. "At my dad's funeral, you said I couldn't trust the people I know."

"Your uncle is keeping something from you. I was with your dad when the commandant arrived on base."

I raised an eyebrow. "Mark flew to North Carolina just to see my dad? When was this?"

"Three days before the accident."

"Why would the commandant of a military academy show up in Jacksonville unannounced?"

Oliver shrugged. "I've been wondering the same thing since the accident. Your dad was upset with him. They argued before the commandant left the base."

"You were there for training, right?"

He nodded.

"Do you think Mark had something to do with his death?"

"I don't know. It was a routine mission. We'd completed the same run dozens of times."

"Tell me what happened that day."

"We were flying over the preserve when the sensors detected an object approaching us. Your dad reacted as quickly as he could. But, unfortunately, there was nothing he could do to save himself."

I started crying all over again, and he wrapped me in his strong embrace. Oliver laid my head on his shoulder, rubbing my back with his palm. His grip tightened with each scream that ripped from my chest. After what felt like hours, I had no tears left.

"I needed that," I whispered as I lifted my head

from his shoulder. "I'm still trying to process his death. Thank you."

He nodded at the letter on my lap. "Are you going to read it?"

I pressed my lips together. "I'm scared."

"It's okay, Grace. Your dad loved you."

I clutched the envelope. "Is this an if I die letter?"

"That would be my guess."

"Did you write one to your family?"

Oliver shook his head, his eyes downcast. "I don't have a family. My parents died when I was nine."

"I'm sorry," I whispered.

"I know what this is like, Grace." He leaned forward, now holding my hand with both of his. "I'm here if you need me."

"I want to wait a little while longer."

Oliver slid his thumb across my cheek to wipe away the last of my tears. "Whenever you're ready."

I hooked my arms around his neck, needing a hug so desperately I didn't care he was my teacher. He was with my father in his final moments and knowing that made me feel closer to him. Clinging to his muscular chest, I nuzzled my nose against his neck. Captain Fox held me for a while before I sat back, our mouths inches apart.

"Have you heard of The Lucaya Group?"

He sat on the pew beside me. "Where did you hear that name?"

"Mark told Cole and Hunter the Founders are happy because The Lucaya Group can't find me at the academy. Do you know what that means?"

Oliver pinched the bridge of his nose between his fingers and looked at the front of the church. "I don't know what he meant in reference to you. But I have heard of them."

"Please, Oliver. I need to know the truth. You're right about the people closest to me hiding something."

"The Lucaya Group is a terrorist organization with cells around the world. As soon as we neutralize one threat, another cell pops up on our radar."

"Why would they want to find me?"

He shrugged. "I wish I had an answer, Grace. Honestly, I have no idea. But if your uncle is in bed with people like The Lucaya Group, you need to run as far away from this school as you can get."

"I don't have anywhere to go and no money. I'm at the Marshalls' mercy until I can figure out an alternative solution."

"Your dad died while he was on active duty. Haven't you received any compensation?"

I shook my head. "Mark said he would handle it."

He sighed. "Don't trust the commandant or his sons."

"Have you heard of the Founders?"

"No."

"Cole said that if my father finds out I'm at the

academy, he will destroy everything their family has built."

He slid his arm behind my back and hugged me. "I'll contact my friend at the NSA and see if he can look into the Marshalls and their connection to The Lucaya Group."

"Mark isn't a terrorist," I muttered. "Neither is Cole."

"You'd be surprised how easy it is for bad people to hide among us."

"What should I do? I can't leave the academy without money or a place to live."

"I can help you, Grace. But you have to be patient. Hang in there until I can find a way to get you off the campus without raising too many suspicions."

I clutched the box and letter in my hand. "Someone chased me through the woods my first weekend at the academy. Do you think they were trying to kill me?"

Oliver shook his head. "No. If The Lucaya Group sent someone, you would be dead. They're trained professionals."

"Why would someone want to kill my dad?"

"I'll find out," he promised. "It's late. You should head back to Bryant Hall."

He rose to his feet, extending his hand to help me up from the pew. "When the time is right, I'll let you know. Just stick it out for a little while longer."

I stuffed the letter into my pocket and tucked the box under my arm. "Thank you. I'll see you in class."

AFTER I RAN BACK to Bryant Hall, I hid the box and letter under a loose floorboard in the back of my closet. The box required a key, and all of my attempts to pry it open were useless. I didn't want to see it every day, to have it in plain sight, taunting me to open it.

Not yet.

I had to find the key first. I still hadn't opened my father's goodbye letter. The wounds were still too new and fresh, and I wanted to wait until I was ready. But would I ever be prepared to read his final words?

The next afternoon, on the way to my final class of the day, two cadets engaged in a heated fist fight at the end of the corridor. At least a dozen cadets surrounded them. YMA had a strict policy against violence. If the staff caught them, they would all get kicked out.

I smiled at the thought, heading in the opposite direction, wanting nothing to do with the other students. They would never consider me one of them, so why bother? Taking the stairs two at a time, I whipped past a group of cadets coming toward me. As usual, they made snide remarks that no longer bothered me.

Whore.

Bitch.

Slut.

Skank.

Barracks Bunny.

They could call me whatever they wanted. The words just rolled down my back.

On the first floor, I ran into my least favorite person at this school. Preston stood beside a locker, his dark eyes burning a hole through me. Of course, Grayson and Rhys were with him. Those three never traveled the halls alone.

This place had its cliques, kind of like high school. Some cadets had attended YMA since middle school and had been friends ever since. Julian and I were the only outliers. At least I had Julian. I was so thankful for his friendship... and whatever was transpiring between us. There was a lot of sexual tension mixed with an incredible amount of desire.

"If it isn't the commandant's charity whore," Preston said to me with fire behind his words.

"You can be my whore, sweetheart." Rhys smirked. "Come wrap those pretty lips around my cock."

I rolled my eyes. "I'd have to find it first."

"Ooh, burn," someone said behind me. "You gonna let her talk to you like that, Rhys?"

Pretty boy Rhys laughed it off. He was every girl's wet dream—except for mine. He could keep his sexy smirks and toned body away from me.

"You couldn't fit my cock in your mouth," Rhys said. "But I'd like to see you try."

The corners of Grayson's mouth lifted into an evil grin. In one swift motion, he wrapped his arm around me and curled my body into his. I elbowed him in the stomach, but he only tightened his grip.

"C'mon, baby. We'll take good care of you."

I swatted at his hand and yelled, "Don't fucking touch me."

Grayson raised my arms above my head and pinned me against the locker. With his mouth inches from mine, I struggled to breathe. Sure, he was hot and built like a soldier, but he was the worst of them all. He scared me the most out of his friends.

I had subdued Rhys at Cole's party over the summer, twisting his arm behind his back with little effort. But I couldn't use any of my moves on Grayson, who now had the upper hand. Everyone in the hall stopped moving, all eyes on me. Students gathered around us, craning their ears to listen to the showdown.

"You want our protection?" Grayson asked, his breath ghosting my lips. "We can make your life easier."

"I don't want anything from any of you."

Rhys leaned against the locker beside me and stroked my cheek with his thumb. "Don't fight us. You won't win."

"Cole and Hunter will kill you."

"Really?" Rhys smirked. "They said you're fair game."

Grayson dipped his hand between my thighs and touched me over top of my pants. "Preston showed us your sex tape. So we already know you can handle all three of us."

I raised my leg to knee him in the balls, but Grayson caught my leg and wrapped it around his back. He lips almost touched mine. My heart raced, my pulse pounding so fast my head spun. I had to get away from them before I passed out from the lack of oxygen to my brain.

"I can't even count how many times I've jerked off to your video," Rhys said as he brushed my hair behind my ear. Then his thumb slid across my bottom lip, dipping into my mouth. I tried to bite his finger, and he laughed, pulling it back. "I can't wait to get you on your knees and riding my cock." A wicked smile graced his perfect lips. "You like taking two cocks at a time, don't you? Hmmm... Like a good little slut."

"I wouldn't fuck you with someone else's vagina."

Rhys tipped his head back and laughed.

"I told you she's trailer trash," Preston interjected. "Nothing but a dumb slut. She thinks she can ride Banks and Marshall's cocks to a payday."

"No, I don't," I shot back, fueled by anger as I fought against my captors. "I fucked them because they know how to make a woman come. I can't say the same for you and your small dick."

"Bitch," Preston growled. "Your pussy is wider than the Grand Canyon." He rested his hand on Rhys' shoulder. "I wouldn't fuck her again if she was the last bitch alive."

"Don't listen to him." Rhys' fingers grazed my cheek. "Be our girl." He tilted his head toward Grayson. "We'll protect you from the wolves."

"Who will protect me from you?"

Grayson released the scariest dark chuckle I'd ever heard. A shiver shot down my arms, dotting my skin with tiny bumps. I would have to be desperate to agree to an arrangement with these idiots. Rhys looked like he would blow your mind in bed. But I wasn't about to find out if my theory held any truth.

I heard a scuffle down the hall but couldn't see past Grayson and Rhys's giant bodies. A few seconds later, hands gripped each of their shoulders, pulling them off me. I blew out a relieved breath when my eyes landed on Cole and Hunter.

I stepped toward them, and Hunter clutched my arm, moving me between him and Cole. His jaw ticked as he studied Preston, Grayson, and Rhys.

"Stay the fuck away from her," Hunter yelled.

"Marshall said she's fair game," Rhys countered. "It's our turn to share her."

"Change of plans," Cole said.

"I'm not a toy for you to pass around." I slipped from Hunter's grasp, shaking my head at him. "You and Cole better make up your minds, or I will take them up on their offer."

I didn't mean it and only wanted them to feel the pain. Cole's mouth twisted in anger, his hands clenched at his sides. Hunter looked equally pissed, grinding his teeth as he studied his competition.

"Let's go, Grace." Hunter's hand moved to my ass, gripping me with possession. "You're going to be late for class."

I peeked up at him. "Please don't man handle me."

He dipped his head down, digging his fingers into my hip. "You're ours, Grace. And they need to know it."

Ignoring his comment, I walked down the hallway and rushed outside, forgetting about all of their games as the doors slammed behind me.

Grace

Julian knocked on my door after dinner with a bucket of supplies in one hand and a mop and broom in the other. He promised to help me whip this room into shape for Friday's inspection.

"You came through." I stepped to the side to let him into the room. "Thank you. You're such a lifesaver."

"No problem, girl. I got your back." He set the bucket on the floor and rested the broom against the wall. "Where do you want to start?"

I scanned the room, which was already neat and organized, apart from the busted furniture and stains on the walls. "Any chance you brought a screwdriver?"

He reached into the bucket and raised a Phillips head.

"Can you fix the drawer handles while I mop the floor?"

He winked. "I am your humble servant."

Julian seemed to know when I needed a laugh. Around him, I smiled all the time. Sometimes, I even forgot about why I was here and all the shit that had happened in the past few weeks.

After I met with Captain Fox, I hid my dad's letter and the wooden box under a floorboard at the back of my closet. A part of me wanted to open the letter with Cole and Hunter at my sides. I also needed to find the key to the box, which I assumed was with my father's belongings that were delivered to Fort Marshall.

Hunter and Cole had protected me from Preston and his friends. I thought that meant they were coming around and would stop pushing me away. But they hadn't spoken to me since.

Julian removed the drawers and set them on my bed while I emptied the supplies from the bucket. I filled it with water from the bathroom, and the wonderful scent of rotten eggs permeated the air. Having a private shower was nice, but it had its disadvantages.

The pipes banged when I showered. The water wasn't all that clear, and the smell was horrific. But it beat showering in the communal bathroom.

I dragged the soapy bucket into the bedroom area. "Did you already clean your room?"

"Yeah." Julian flipped the wooden drawer over and removed the handle with the screwdriver. "Your boy, Marshall, is such a neat freak. The place is always spotless. He threatened me under penalty of death when I moved in with them. I don't even sleep under the covers. That's the trick to passing inspection every time." He glanced over at me and winked. "Do the same, Hale."

"I'm not messy." I lifted the mop and dunked it into the water, ringing it out. "My dad would never tolerate an unorganized room. He's the one who taught me how to make my bed. He would stand over me and say, *Hospital corners, Gracie.*"

"When I was home from school, the staff did everything. I never had to lift a finger."

I laughed. "I'm surprised you know how to use a screwdriver."

He flipped the drawer over, grinning at me as if he were proud of his handiwork. "All done. I might be a rich boy, but I'm resourceful."

"I can see that."

Julian dropped the tool on my bed and slowly approached me. "What's next on your honey do list?"

I chuckled at his comment. "You saying you want to be my man, Archer?"

He licked his lips. "I'll be anything you want me to be."

"Can you sweep the other side of the room?"

Without a word, Julian did as I asked. We kept ourselves busy for the next thirty minutes until the floor shone. I felt good about inspection. There wasn't much

Cole or Hunter could say about the place. It wasn't the Ritz Carlton, but it looked presentable.

"I'm passing inspection."

He beamed with delight. "Damn right, girl. Like I would let you fail because of those bastards. You're not going anywhere."

I put the mop in the bucket and leaned it against the wall, so I could join Julian on the bed. He cupped his knees with his hands, leaning forward to study me, like he was committing every feature to memory.

"I have to clean the shower," I said.

"I'll help you."

He followed me into the bathroom. I reached into the dirty shower and held my breath when I turned on the water.

Julian covered his mouth, speaking between his fingers. "What is that smell?"

"The stench of rot," I joked. "It's from not using the water for a long time and won't go away. Can you grab the scrub brushes and the bleach?"

He nodded, leaving the room for a few seconds before he returned with the products in hand. I took them from him and dumped half the bottle onto the grimy tile and got on my hands and knees to scrub the shower. Julian sank to his knees beside me, and with some elbow grease, he helped me cleanse this dump.

By the time we finished, water soaked us from head

to toe, but at least the bathroom was clean. I rose to my feet with Julian's help, and I fell into his chest. He hooked his arm around my back and smiled.

I loved when he smiled, because it was a real one that reached his eyes. I moved in front of the sink and washed the bleach and dirt from my hands. Then I moved out of the way for Julian, who stared at me in the mirror as he ran his hands under the sink.

Julian lifted his shirt over his head, exposing his tanned, muscular abdomen. I bit the inside of my cheek. He had dark tattoos that started under his collarbone and trailed down his chest, dipping below the sexy V that peeked out from his boxer briefs.

Damn, he looked good.

We were friends, but when you had friends like him...

I leaned my back against the sink and checked him out, as he had done to me dozens of times. My chest rose and fell, my breathing labored from all the pent-up sexual frustration coursing through my body. The air between us crackled with electricity, the spark of energy gliding up my arms.

He moved his hand to my waist and whispered, "Stop me."

"Not a chance."

His lips moved against mine, his tongue slipping into my mouth, soft and slow and with just the right amount of pressure. I hooked my arms around his neck, and he lifted me off my feet, setting me down on the counter. He moved between my spread thighs, his fingers grazing my hot skin. Since he was shirtless, I stripped off my wet tank top and threw it across the room.

Julian kissed my neck, leaving a trail of kisses between my breasts, all the way to my belly button. He stopped moving right above my pussy, and I wondered if he could smell my desire. Tugging on the waistband of my shorts, he peeked up at me. Dark strands of hair covered his forehead when he bent his head down and licked my skin. I writhed beneath him, desperate for him to touch me.

Slipping my fingers through his hair, I tugged on the ends. "Julian, I want you to kiss me everywhere."

He grinned at the challenge, then inched my shorts lower, taking my panties with them. I reached out and rolled my thumb across his lower lip, and he sucked my finger into his mouth. A sexy expression crossed his handsome face, causing my insides to melt. I moved my hand to the back of his head, encouraging him to keep going.

Julian ripped off my shorts and panties. He bit his lip and sucked in a deep breath, right before he split me down the middle with his tongue. I screamed from the intense wave of pleasure rocking me to the core. Draping my legs over his strong shoulders, he drove his tongue into my pussy, going deeper and deeper until my entire body trembled.

"Julian," I moaned. "Oh, fuck. Mmm… Oh, my God, that feels so good."

He glanced up at me, making slow, circular motions over my clit with his thumb. With his other hand, he plunged two fingers inside me, massaging my inner walls, stretching me out. Desperate for more of his tongue, I rocked my hips, tugging harder on his hair. I pushed my bra out of the way and rubbed my thumb over my nipple. Julian's eyes widened, a sexy look plastered on his face.

I screamed his name, this time louder than the last. He took me to new heights, satiating desires I thought no one would fulfill other than my best friends. But I was making new friends. Apparently, I wasn't capable of not having a sexual relationship with mine.

Julian shattered my existence with each flick of his tongue. And when I thought I couldn't handle anymore, I came for a second time on his tongue, my entire body on fire from his skilled touch.

He breathed over my hot flesh for a second, his eyes fixed on me. "Dammit, Grace. You've fucking ruined me."

I chuckled, then lowered my legs to the counter. "No, you destroyed me. Wow, Julian. That was…"

He stood between my legs and wiped his mouth with the back of his hand. My eyes lowered to his cock, which poked through his sweatpants. I shoved his pants and boxers down and fisted his cock. His eyes slammed shut as a groan escaped his lips. Using some of my wetness to lubricate his cock, I slid my hand up and down his long shaft. His eyes popped open, then lowered to my hand wrapped around his length.

"I don't have a condom," he said with annoyance dripping from his tone.

"We have all year, Julian. Tonight, let's just get to know each other's bodies."

He grabbed the back of my head and kissed me, groaning into my mouth as I stroked his big cock. I scooted forward on the counter so I could rub my wetness against him. Julian's eyes opened for a second, and then he kissed me again, harder and with more passion than the last one.

"Fuck, Grace," he muttered between kisses. "Your pussy feels so good. I can't wait to be inside you."

I increased my speed, and his legs shook mine. Julian gripped my biceps for support, his entire body trembling as he came on my stomach. He rested his forehead against mine, moved his palms to each side of my legs, and then he kissed me. It was quick, just a peck that left me wanting more.

"I can't even remember the last time I came that hard," he whispered, his head lowered as he steadied his breathing.

"Me neither. We should get in the shower."

He glanced down at his cum on my stomach and then stepped out from between my thighs to turn on the water. Throwing his hand into the stall to test the temperature, he looked over at me and waggled his eyebrows.

I laughed. "You're too much."

"Is that a bad thing?"

I hopped off the counter and stood beside him. "No, not at all. I like you just the way you are."

After we kissed in the shower and made each other come again, we towel dried our bodies and got into my bed naked. We used each other's body heat for warmth, and after a few minutes of kissing and touching, I had all the heat I needed.

Hours passed before my eyelids fluttered, and I could no longer fight sleep. Julian laid on his back, and I curled up against his warm body and slept on his chest.

MY EYES SHOT open from the loud bang on the door. Heart racing, I sat up and clutched my chest, wondering where the noise came from, until I heard a voice outside of my room.

"Open up, Hale," Cole ordered. "It's time for inspection."

"Fuck, fuck, fuck," I whispered, freaking the fuck out over Julian naked on the bed beside me.

We were so busy making out last night, I forgot to set an alarm and hide the cleaning supplies. The mop was still in the bucket across the room, the broom propped up against the wall. I slid off the bed, wrapping the sheet around my body, and whisper-yelled for Julian to hide in the closet.

"It's no use," he told me. "They're going to check every inch of the place."

"Fuck," I whined.

Cole banged on the door again. "Open up, Hale, or I'm coming in there."

"What am I going to do? He's going to fail me. I'll probably get written up for having you in my room."

"There's nothing we can do. We have to face this together."

Julian quickly dressed in his boxer briefs and sweatpants. His shirt was still wet and on the floor in the bathroom. I rushed over to the closet and lifted my uniform off the hanger. But before I could set it on the bed, the door flew open and hit the wall.

Cole stood in the doorway with his hands on his hips, his eyes moving between Julian and me. Of course, our platoon commander had keys to our rooms.

His face contorted with a sinister expression that

chilled me to the core. "What the fuck is going on here?" Cole demanded.

"It's not her fault," Julian said as he approached my former best friend. "We overslept."

Cole stepped forward, dressed in his uniform, his short white-blond hair styled with gel. "I'm writing both of you up for insubordination," he said, leveling Julian with a hard look. "The commandant will hear about this. And you've just lost fifty points for our platoon. I hope you're happy." He grinned with a sick satisfaction. "You will be on everyone's kill list. You won't last through the weekend."

"We didn't have sex," I said, as if it was some consolation to soothe his anger.

Cole bent down to meet my height. "I know what you look like after you come. You can't lie to me, Grace."

I tightened my grip on the sheet, though it concealed little since it was sheer and white. "Jealous, sir?"

His breath slid across my lips when he spoke. "Not a fucking chance, Hale. Now get fucking dressed." He pointed his finger at Julian. "And you, get the fuck out."

Julian shoved a hand through his dark hair and chuckled. "Grace had it right the first time. You're jealous, Marshall." He stepped to Cole, which wasn't the best idea when he was this mad. "She's not yours anymore."

Cole shoved his palms into Julian's bare chest, and he staggered to the side. The two cadets closed the distance, standing nose-to-nose, about to rip each other's heads off. Unsure of what to do, I poked my head into the hallway. Hunter was midway down the row, inspecting rooms on the other side of the floor.

"Hunter," I called out.

Dozens of eyes shot in my direction, and then Hunter looked at me.

"Come here, please. Before they kill each other."

He said something to the cadet beside him before rushing toward me, his gaze lowering to the sheet. "Why are you not dressed?"

I opened the door wider to reveal the fight taking place between Julian and Cole.

Hunter's jaw clenched. "Did you fuck him?"

I shook my head. "No, but he spent the night."

"What the fuck were you thinking, Grace?"

Hunter crossed the room to pull Cole and Julian apart. A few minutes passed before the commotion died down. Julian kissed my cheek and promised to see me later, then left in a hurry.

"Get dressed," Hunter ordered as Cole entered the bathroom to take an inventory of everything that was out of place. "Now. Before he kills you."

"Cole wouldn't hurt me."

"No, but I would not mess with him right now."
Hunter closed the door and locked it, nodding at the
closet. "Put on your uniform."

"Look, I know you're pissed because you don't like
Julian."

"You couldn't even pass inspection," Cole said with
an attitude as he came out of the bathroom.

"This isn't about the inspection, Cole."

"I told you to stay away from Archer," he shouted.
"I told you he's a liar. And you let him fuck you?"

"We didn't have sex." I threw my hands in the air.
"Stop saying that."

He crossed the room in a second and grabbed my
waist. The sheet slipped from my body and fell onto
the floor. Cole's eyes dropped to my bare breasts. So
did Hunter's.

"Why did you let him touch you?"

"It's none of your business, Cole. We're not friends
anymore. You don't have a say in who I'm friends
with."

"Why, Grace? Of all the people, you chose him?"

"Well, maybe if you two would take your heads out
of your asses and stop pushing me away, I wouldn't
have to find new friends."

Hunter scrubbed his hand across his jaw and
sighed.

Cole remained expressionless, though his anger was

clear from the coldness in his blue eyes. "How could you let him touch you?"

"If you were still fucking me, I wouldn't need to go elsewhere." I looked at Hunter. "But seeing as both of you have abandoned me, I don't have many options."

Cole's big hand moved from my hip to right beneath my breast. He massaged the skin with his fingers, as if he were thinking about touching me in other places.

"I wish I never met you."

He gritted his teeth. "Don't say that."

"I mean it."

"No, you don't," Hunter interjected.

"Julian is really good with his hands and tongue," I said to annoy them. "He made me come so hard I saw stars."

"That's it," Cole snapped, dropping his hand from my body. He turned his back to me. "Because of your stupidity, you have just lost your platoon one hundred points. Get dressed, Hale. If you're not in the hallway in full uniform in thirty seconds, you'll lose another fifty points for every second you're late."

Hunter breathed through his nose, unable to meet my gaze. I'd never seen him so disappointed in me. "You're fucked, Grace. This was stupid. I hope an orgasm was worth losing the War Games for us this early in the year."

"We won't lose," I challenged. "I will make up the points."

"Unless you blow every professor on campus," Cole said with sarcasm in his tone, "you're not making up the points, which means one of us will have to do it for you. Watch your back, Grace. Once the sharks sniff blood, they go in for the kill."

They left in a hurry, slamming the door so hard a wave of anxiety slithered down my spine. I was so fucked. All because I wanted to get fucked.

Grace

Our entire platoon hated my guts. Each time I walked past the scoreboard in the hallway, docking our team one hundred points because of me, they shouted insults. People yelled for me to go home.

On Friday night, I waited for Julian. And then again on Saturday. He was a no-show for breakfast and then again at lunch and dinner. Either Cole kept Julian locked in his room, or he was avoiding me because of the inspection incident.

My depression worsened with all the time I spent alone. With each hour that passed, I considered opening my dad's letter, wondering if it would bring me some comfort. But I wasn't ready for closure. Sometimes, you needed to feel the pain and let it fester deep in your heart before you could move on.

So that was my plan for now.

On Sunday, I started packing my bags. I didn't belong here, and there was no way I would last another week, let alone the semester. No one would have noticed if I slipped out of my room in the middle of the night. But I doubted I could get past the guards posted at the front gate. Students could not leave the school grounds without permission.

Julian was still AWOL at every meal on Sunday. We were not required to eat meals together on R&R days. Still, I wondered if I was the cause. If he wanted me to feel the sting of his rejection, I received the message. Loud and clear.

Before bed on Sunday night, I laid out a fresh uniform and grabbed a pair of PT clothes to wear as pajamas. Since we had to workout together bright and early each morning, I didn't see the point in sleeping in anything else. This way I could crawl out of bed, prepared to start my hellish morning.

My hair was a mess from sweating and sleeping for most of the day, so I headed into the bathroom. I stripped out of my dirty clothes and reached into the stall shower. The knobs turned with some resistance, the pipes groaning like an old engine backfiring. Brown water spilled from the shower head, then the scent of eggs filled the room.

I turned off the shower and dressed. There was a communal bathroom at the center of the floor. All cadets shared apartment suites with their team, but not all suites had a private bathroom. I grabbed my shower caddy and poked my head out the door. The hallway was silent at this hour. If I was quick about it, I could sneak into the shower unnoticed and get out.

Five minutes. That was all I needed to scrub my

skin and wash my hair. Without a second to spare, I stepped into the hallway and crept toward the bathroom. I felt like a kid sneaking out of bed in the middle of the night to eat junk food. Any minute, a cadet could open his door. What if someone was already in the bathroom?

I entered the communal bathroom, which was clean for a bunch of boys. There were rows of lockers to my left and toilets to my right. I walked down the aisle until I reached another bank of lockers. Metal racks hung on the walls, stocked with plush bath towels in the school's colors. I plucked one from the bunch and hung it on one of the hooks by the showers.

A dozen shower heads encased in glass spanned the length of the exterior wall. I set the shower caddy on the floor, gulping down my fear. In and out, I took a deep breath and turned the knob. The pipes didn't cry out, and thankfully the water wasn't brown or smelled like eggs, which was a welcome relief.

I peeled off my clothes and dropped them onto the bench, taking one last look into the room. Quickly, I lathered shampoo in my hair and washed it out. Then I got to work soaping up my body, afraid to waste more time than necessary.

Feeling like a new woman, I flicked off the water and lifted the shower caddy from the floor. I reached for the towel I'd hung on the wall.

What the fuck?

Blinking the water from my eyes, I stared at the empty hook in horror. There was no way someone snuck into the room, and yet, someone had stolen my shit. I checked the bench where I'd left my clothes. Of course, it was empty.

Shit, shit, shit...

I left the caddy on the bench and looked for a towel, but the entire rack was empty. *Motherfuckers.* How did those assholes get into the bathroom without me seeing or hearing them? With only one exit and zero options, I had one play to make.

And I had to make it fast.

My heart pounded so hard and fast I could hear it beating in my ears. Tears burned my eyes, but I refused to let a single drop fall. I'd been through a lot of shit in my life. I had endured years of being carted from one place to the next, and I never complained.

Like my father had taught me, I adapted to my situation and learned how to overcome the obstacles at each new duty station. In the past, kids on base tried to sabotage me. One girl even went as far as locking me in a closet so I couldn't take the final exam. But I'd never endured this kind of bullshit from boys.

Yet, these were men.

I searched the room for a scrap of fabric, anything at all I could use for a towel. Those bastards took my clothes. But I wouldn't let them see me sweat. They would never see me beg. Their games were stupid and childish, and I wouldn't let them win.

So I resorted to my only choice. I had to hide my lady parts from those deviant cadets. This was what they wanted. To see me naked and vulnerable, to look stupid and pathetic.

Not a chance.

I stopped in front of the paper towel dispenser and tugged on the paper, twirling it around my naked body. After wrapping myself like a mummy, I stood in front of the mirror and inspected my appearance.

I had dark circles under my eyes from the lack of sleep. My pale skin looked somewhat bruised from enduring the harsh training. I went as hard as the guys, undeterred by my limitations.

Holding my head high, I walked out of the bathroom and into the hallway. As I expected, the cadets waited for me, lined up down the left side of the hallway with their eyes on me.

"Amazing Grace," they sang in unison, "how sweet the sound…"

All of them stared through me, singing the words to *Amazing Grace* to taunt me.

"You're so unoriginal," I shouted at them. "Amazing Grace? Really?"

Even though they glared at me with pure hatred, a few of them inspected my towel arrangement, their eyes appraising my body with desire.

"Give back my clothes," I said to Rhys.

He crossed his arms over his bare chest and smirked. Since he ignored me, I went down the line, sizing up the rest of them. There had to be at least thirty men gaping at me like they wanted to fuck me. Most of their stares were brutal and cruel, full of venom and hatred.

"Let's play capture the barracks bunny," Grayson yelled, and a shiver rushed down my arms.

I inched down the hall toward my living quarters, with my hands raised in front of me and balled into fists. "Stay the fuck away from me," I warned, even though I couldn't take all of them in a fight.

"She talks a good game when her boyfriends are around," Preston taunted. "But she's not so tough now."

"What the fuck is going on out here?"

I breathed a sigh of relief at the sound of Cole's voice. Despite his current hatred for me, I knew he would never let these assholes hurt me.

"Why are you out of your rooms after 2200 hours?" Cole's eyes wavered as he walked down the row. "You know the rules. Back to bed."

No one owned up to their little stunt.

Cole looked at me like I was as insignificant as bird shit on his window. "What the fuck are you wearing, Hale?"

"It's not my fault. They took my clothes and towel while I was in the shower."

"You're breaking curfew," he shot back. "What are you doing out of your quarters and in the common bathroom?"

"Oh, so you're going to yell at me for taking a shower? How about you give your buddies a hard time for stealing my shit?"

"We did no such thing," someone said behind me. "She's a liar. Just another barracks bunny who wants attention."

I glanced over my shoulder and pointed my finger at him. "No, I'm not. Don't you dare call me that." Then I looked up at Cole. "You need to do something about them."

His gaze moved down the line of cadets. "I have no proof of any wrongdoing. I can't punish my men without it."

"We used to be best friends, Cole. What is wrong with you?"

"You don't belong here, Grace," he said with a dead look in his eyes. "It's time for you to go home."

Home?

I didn't have a home anymore.

Hell, I never really had one.

I'd always considered Fort Marshall the closest thing I ever had to home because all of my favorite childhood memories took place there.

243

I folded my arms over my chest, though that didn't stop Cole from taking a peek at my nipples tearing through the wet paper. "What have I done to make you hate me this much?" Cole's jaw clenched at my words. "You want me gone? I get it. I know I don't belong here. But I'm not going anywhere, so get used to it."

"I had nothing to do with this." He dipped his head down until his lips were inches from mine. "If I wanted to get you naked, I would have gone about it in other ways."

I shoved my palms into his chest. "You're the worst kind of bully, Cole."

"Get back to your room before I punish you for insubordination."

I tipped my head back and laughed. "Your threats mean nothing. Write me up all you want, asshole. I'm not in the wrong." I pointed at the cadets to our left. "They started this. How about you punish them?"

The corner of his delicious mouth turned up into a crooked grin that made him look even sexier. "Marshall Law differs from the YMA Code of Conduct. You're in my world now, Grace. What I say goes. If you fall out of line again, your punishment will impact the platoon. And you won't like the consequences."

"Hey, dickhead," a male voice boomed.

I spun around, relieved to see Julian racing down the hall toward us. Almost everyone on our floor was awake and staring at us.

Where had he disappeared to all weekend?

"Leave her alone," Julian said as he approached us.

"Go back to your room," Cole ordered.

"No. Fuck you," Julian challenged. He stood behind me, and I looked up at him with tired eyes, so damn thankful to see him. "Does it make you feel like a big man to gang up on the only girl at this school? I bet Daddy Commandant doesn't know what you're doing to her."

"Stay out of this," Cole shot back, his top lip quivering. His eyes were wide and intense, like they were ready to bug out of his head. "And stay away from Hale."

"She's a member of my platoon. And unlike you and the rest of the cadets, I take the oath I made seriously." Julian pulled his shirt over his head, and I practically drooled at the sight of his washboard abdomen. He handed it to me. "Put this on, Grace."

With Cole shielding my front and Julian blocking my back, I slipped my arms into the holes and pulled it over my head. It was a black YMA Athletics shirt with the school's gold logo. The fabric smelled like a mixture of Julian's spicy cologne and sweat. I loved the way he smelled, like a man after a hard day of work.

Julian curled his long fingers around my bicep. "C'mon, Grace. Time for bed."

"And you think what you're doing is any different?" Cole asked him.

He sneered. "Afraid of a little competition, Marshall?"

Cole glared at him.

I walked into my bedroom with Julian. The other guys would assume the worst, but I didn't care. I was happy to be alone with someone normal, someone who didn't get joy from making a woman feel like shit.

"Are you okay?" Julian asked me.

I nodded. "Yeah, I'm fine. Thanks for helping me out."

"Grace, you don't look fine." He hovered over me, all six feet three inches of muscle. His delicious scent invaded my nostrils as he looked down at me, and for a moment, I wanted to kiss him. "I have three sisters. There's no way you're okay. Did any of those assholes touch you?"

I shook my head. "No, but if Cole hadn't shown up, who knows what would have happened."

"He was behind it," Julian shot back.

"I don't think so. I've known Cole since we were kids. That's not his style. He would find another way to get rid of me."

Julian cupped my cheek. "Are you sure you're okay?"

"It's behind me now."

"They won't stop until you leave the school."

"I know. And I won't let them force me out. My dad attended YMA. He said some of his greatest

246

memories were at this school. He also said it was hard being the only scholarship kid. But he had my uncle Mark on his side. And I have you. So I know it's going to be okay because he survived, and I will too."

"It's not the same," Julian pointed out. "You're not just a scholarship kid."

"They're intimidated by a girl. That says more about them than it does me."

"I'm not intimidated by you," he said in a deep voice that rolled down my arms. "You impress the hell out of me. Most men couldn't endure the shit they have put you through. And yet, you're still here, defying the odds just to spite them."

I reached under Julian's long shirt and grabbed wads of paper towels from my skin. "Sorry." I flung the paper into the trash can. "I know this isn't very lady-like, but I can't stand having wet paper stuck to my skin for another second."

He turned his back to me. "I can leave to give you some privacy."

"No. Will you stay with me?"

"Whatever you want, Grace. I'm yours to command."

I finished ripping the wet paper towels off my skin and took off his shirt, setting it on top of the dresser. I paired a black sports bra with a navy tank top and stepped into a pair of panties and spandex shorts.

I handed Julian his shirt. "Thanks for having my back."

He pushed the shirt into my chest. "Keep it. Never know when you might need it."

For a moment, I let my eyes linger on his bare chest. He had dark tattoos starting beneath his collarbone to the sexy V that dipped beneath his mesh basketball shorts. I licked my lips, and he stared at me with equal intensity.

"Where were you this weekend?"

He tensed at my question, shifting his weight uncomfortably. "Dealing with family drama."

"You were allowed to go home?"

"My sisters needed me." Julian ran a hand through his dark hair and turned away. "Anyway, I should go. You need your rest for tomorrow."

"No, stay. I haven't slept well without Sarge in bed with me."

His eyebrows lifted. "Who's Sarge? You got a secret boyfriend I don't know about?"

I chuckled. "No. Sarge is my English bulldog. She's staying at the commandant's house while I'm here. I miss her. It's been hard getting to sleep without her by my side."

He extended his arm toward my bed. "Get in. I'll get the lights."

I folded back the sheets and slipped beneath them as Julian turned out the lights. A few seconds later, he crossed the room, the mattress dipping from his weight. He rolled onto his side, so we were facing each other. I could feel his breath on my lips, but could not make out all of his handsome features in the darkness.

"I'm happy I met you, Julian."

His hand covered mine on the bed. "Me too, Grace."

"I'm guessing your sisters are the reason you always stick up for me."

"Yeah." He sighed. "They're younger than me and are always getting into trouble."

"What are their names?"

"Savanna and Sawyer are twins and the youngest. Ella is a year younger than me. She keeps getting involved with losers."

"Did you get everything sorted?"

"I'm dealing with it. Close your eyes and try to get some sleep."

"Can you turn the lock on your way out? I don't want any of those creeps coming in after you leave?"

I also couldn't afford to let him spend the night, not after losing one hundred points for First Platoon.

"I'll do you one better," Julian said in a hushed tone. "After you fall asleep, I'll stand watch outside your door. Don't worry. I won't let them touch you."

"Thank you, Julian," I whispered, right before I passed out.

Grace

I got into formation with my platoon and entered the mess hall. My stomach rumbled from the scent of chicken and vegetables. We took turns getting our food and ate in silence. Midway through dinner, Cole stood at the end of the table, sizing up our platoon for the weakest link. I was sure that was me, even though I didn't think so.

He surprised me by calling on a cadet five seats from me. O'Leary stood, his eyes on the wall as Cole stared at him.

"What year did Richard York found the academy?"

The cadet cleared his throat. "Eighteen ninety-seven, sir."

"Which month?"

Arms straight at his sides, he stared into the expanse of the room. "August, sir."

"On which day," Cole said with an attitude.

"August twelfth eighteen ninety-seven, sir."

Cole went down the line, choosing random cadets and firing off one question after the other about the school. We had to memorize the York Military

Academy Cadet Handbook by heart. Failure to learn everything about the school would lead to a deduction in points for the platoon. I'd been reading it nightly from the moment I received my packet. It was the one thing in my room the cadets didn't trash.

"Hale," Cole boomed from the end of the table.

I dropped my fork onto my plate and glanced in his direction.

"Rise and recite the phonetic alphabet."

My mouth opened in surprise, but I knew better than to challenge my commanding officer. His request wasn't hard. So I did as he instructed and stood to my full height. The cadets stared at me, some with interest, others with their usual hateful smirks.

I stood with my hands at my sides and cleared my throat. "Alpha, Bravo, Charlie, Delta, Echo, Foxtrot…"

By the time I reached Zulu, I was out of breath.

Cole's jaw clenched. "Now say it backward."

I lifted an eyebrow at him.

"Now, Hale," he yelled. "No one leaves this table until you finish."

"Yes, sir," I said through clenched teeth. "Zulu, Yankee, X-ray, Whiskey, Victor, Uniform, Tango…"

I stopped for a moment to think, and someone said, "Sahara."

When they said it, I didn't even think and blurted out, "Sahara," instead of Sierra.

Knowing I screwed up, I drew a breath from

between my teeth and shook my head at the black-haired cadet who yelled out the wrong word.

"Start from the beginning, Hale," Cole ordered. "Screw up again, and your entire platoon will pay the price."

Oh, fuck.

Everyone already hated me.

Nerves shot down my arms, settling deep into my bones. "Zulu," I said, my voice trembling. "Yankee, X-ray, Whiskey, Victor, Uniform, Tango, Sierra, Romeo…"

I made it to the end of the list, ready to celebrate my victory when I tripped on my words and said Julia instead of Juliet.

Dammit, I was so close.

"I meant Juliet," I corrected.

"You failed, Hale."

I dared a glance at Cole, who grinned like a maniac. Hands on his narrow hips, he pushed out his thick chest. Hunter pressed his lips together, a grim expression on his face. He seemed saddened for me, probably because he knew what would come next.

"I know the phonetic alphabet," I said in my defense.

"You had two chances, Hale." Cole gave me a taunting look. "Congratulations, you've lost another fifty points for your platoon."

Whispers spread down the table, all eyes aimed at

me—their enemy. The cadets shot daggers in my direction. They wanted me out of their school as badly as Cole.

A KNOCK on the door sent a wave of panic down my spine. Who the hell was at my door at this hour? Nothing good could come from letting any of the cadets into my room.

Holding my breath, I inched toward the door and cringed when the person knocked again, this time louder than before.

"Grace," he said in a soft tone. "Let me in."

It was Julian.

I pulled the door open. He stood in the entryway, with his hand on the wall, and beamed a smile at me. "You gonna let me in, or should I stand out here until we get in trouble for breaking curfew?"

I stepped to the side to make room for his big body. "How did you leave your room without Cole riding your ass?"

"I snuck out when he was in his room with Hunter." Julian closed the door and shook his head. "There's something strange with those two."

"Like what?"

He rolled his shoulders. "I don't know. They're close. A little too close if you ask me."

"They're best friends," I said in their defense.

"I've never had friends like that."

I sat on the bed and tucked my feet under my butt, leaving plenty of room for Julian to sit. "What did they do?"

He scooted closer to me on the mattress. "They spend a lot of time in each other's bedrooms."

I laughed. "Let me guess. You think they're gay?"

"I'm not sure what to think. Brax seems to keep to himself most of the time. He's usually in his room, blasting music and drawing on his contraband iPad. That thing goes everywhere with him."

"You know about us, right?" I figured it was time to clear the air. "Cole, Hunter, and me."

He lifted a curious eyebrow. "So they are into each other?"

I shook my head. "No, they're into me. Well, they *were* into me. It's a long story."

Julian dipped his head down, and dark strands of hair fell in front of his eyes. "Can I tell you a secret?"

"Sure. Let's hear it."

"I've never had a friend before."

My eyes widened at his confession. "Are you serious? But you're like twenty-one."

"I never stayed in one place long enough to make friends. Not until now."

Silence passed over the room. I studied his gorgeous face, thanking God for sending him to me in my moment of need. Julian was like my shining beacon of hope at this school. Without him, I would not have survived some of the worst days.

"I'm glad you're here."

He smiled, then slid his hand on top of mine. "Me too."

My nipples hardened to peaks from his careful inspection of my face. Thankfully, the shirt was too big for him to see the effect his sexy smirk had on my body. I thought about running my hands through his messy hair, leaning forward to kiss his lips.

Just one more taste.

That was all I wanted.

Before I could make a move, Julian said, "So now that we're sharing secrets, how did you end up with Cole and Hunter?"

"We never dated," I clarified.

"You're important to them. I see how they watch you. I've overheard them talking about you."

"What did they say?"

"Cole wants you to leave YMA."

I rolled my eyes. "Yeah, that's nothing new. He's made it clear I don't belong."

"Hunter talks about your ass a lot," he said with laughter in his tone. "Like more than a normal amount. I can't say I blame him. I love your ass."

I chuckled. "Hunter's obsessed with me. That's why I invited him to join us."

"So you were with Marshall first?"

"For years before Hunter entered the equation. It started when we were kids. Back then, it was just a crush. In high school, Cole gave me my first kiss. He was my first everything."

"Doesn't sound like you had much of a friendship."

"No, we did."

Cole always had my back.

He was the first person to defend me.

"Sounds like he thinks of you as his possession."

"In some ways, I guess. He used to be very protective of me. Like he was afraid someone would steal me if he didn't watch over me."

"I heard Hunter and Cole talking," he said in a hushed tone. "That's why I'm here."

I leaned forward, our mouths so close I felt his breath on my lips. "What did you hear?"

"They said the Founders want her here."

My brows furrowed in confusion. "I overheard them saying that at the commandant's house. Do you know what it means?"

"No clue." Julian leaned against the wall and kicked out his long legs. His black boots hung off the edge of the bed. "I thought you might know."

"Nope." I moved beside him, using the wall for support, and released a deep breath. "If the Founders —whoever they are—want me at this school, then why is Cole trying so hard to get rid of me?"

"He thinks they made a terrible decision by letting you come here."

"What does Hunter think?"

Julian turned his head to the side. "He wants you to stay."

"How did they sound? Do you think I'm not safe here?"

"Stay." He held my hand against the mattress, his warm fingers weaving between mine, sending shock waves down my arm. "I don't care what Marshall wants. I'm not ready to let you go. I will do anything in my power to protect you from the other cadets."

"You're the only person who's been nice to me at this school." I squeezed his hand and smiled. "Thank you, Julian."

"As I said, I've never had a friend until now. So I don't care if everyone hates me. I'm used to being the villain."

"Wouldn't you rather be the hero?"

"Nah." He laughed. "Villains have more fun."

"But the hero gets the girl."

Julian slid his other hand beneath my chin, tilting my head until our eyes met. "Do they?"

And then he kissed me.

His lips were soft and warm, and he tasted like mint. As our tongues tangled, I moaned in his mouth, so damn horny and worked up. I wanted him to satisfy the ache in my core. He kissed me hard, and with so much passion, my lips burned. I climbed onto his lap. Julian massaged my breast over top of my bra, tugging on the fabric. He was like a hungry beast attacking my body.

I moaned when he twisted my nipple between his fingers and bit my bottom lip. "Julian," I whimpered between kisses, rocking my hips to meet his, desperate to rub my clit against his very hard cock.

I leaned forward, throwing my arms around his neck. We kissed and kissed some more until it chapped our lips and we were out of air. Julian didn't push me to take things any farther. He made me come just by pinching my nipples. It was one of the best orgasms of my life, and he barely touched me.

It was late by the time we flicked off the lights and curled up beside each other in my bed. Julian draped his arm over me and hugged me from behind. Exhausted from kissing and the long day, I closed my eyes. His lips brushed my ear, and his head rested on my pillow. It felt so good to be intimate with someone other than Cole and Hunter.

"I'll leave after you fall asleep," Julian said in a hushed tone.

Within minutes, I drifted to thoughts of Julian swimming through my head.

I AWOKE to a loud bang followed by several sets of footsteps. The sound approached my bed, though, in the darkness, I could only see shapes. Julian sat up, more aware of his surroundings than me, and jumped out of bed.

He raised his fists in the air as several figures approached him, ready to fight. "Get the fuck out," Julian yelled before he threw a punch.

It landed, but I couldn't tell where in the darkness. The other person groaned and cursed under his breath. A familiar voice I recognized.

"Hunter Banks," I yelled. "You better turn on the light and stop fucking around."

As Julian fought Hunter, strong arms wrapped around me, lifting me off the bed. I swatted at his bulky muscles, which did little to help my situation. He was too strong and had me in a death grip against his chest. Judging by his feel and smell, it was Cole.

"Put me down, Cole Marshall, or I will kick your ass."

"C'mon, I got her," Cole said to his friends.

Julian thew another punch at Hunter before we stepped into the dimly lit hallway. I'd expected others waiting for us, but the corridor was silent at this hour.

"Cole, put me down." I tugged on his arm as he walked toward the stairs. "This isn't funny. Where are you taking me?"

"There's no use fighting me, Grace. You know I will win."

I heard footsteps smack the tiled floor behind us. I couldn't see over Cole's shoulder, but I assumed it was Julian, Hunter, and probably Brax. He was usually around when my cadets were doing dumb shit.

Cole raced down the stairs as if I weighed nothing and didn't stop until we were in the Quad. My jaw dropped in horror at the sight of our entire platoon in formation, their shadows cast on the grass by the moonlight. It had to be at least two or three o'clock in the morning.

"They have you to thank for not getting any sleep," Cole said with a chuckle. "Isn't that right, boys? You want to show Hale your appreciation for what comes next."

A few people answered him in groans.

Cole set me on the grass in front of the group so I faced everyone. The evil glares shot in my direction caused me to tremble with fear. I looked away, unable to meet their sharp gazes. Hunter shoved Julian into the line. He outranked Hunter and was the same rank as Cole, but Julian didn't protest.

Staring hard at Cole, Julian clenched his jaw. "What do you want, Marshall?"

"What were you doing in Hale's room after curfew?"

A resounding echo of chatter filled the air, my

name a whisper on their lips. I was so stupid to let Julian sleep in bed with me. I blamed it on the orgasm and the exhaustion, and the fact I finally felt safe enough around another person to lower my guard.

"It wasn't her fault," Julian protested. "If you want to punish someone, it should be me."

Cole stood straight, arms behind his back, dressed in black fatigues. "We're here tonight because Hale couldn't say the phonetic alphabetic correctly." His eyes swept over the cadets. "Let this be a reminder to all of you to be prepared at all times."

Cole ordered us to do jumping jacks. My limbs ached from cadet training, but I pushed through the pain. Two hundred jumping jacks into our punishment, Cole and Hunter grabbed hoses from the side of the building. They blasted the group with cold water, and with the breeze blowing off the ocean, it felt like winter had come early.

The cadets hissed and growled with each second of painful torture, their hardened stares aimed at me. A ripple of fear shot down my spine. I would never be one of them. They would never accept me, even if I passed the cadet training. So why was I still here? Maybe I should have taken Cole's advice and left.

"You're done at this school," one cadet said as he passed by me.

I didn't recognize him or his friends who spit at my feet. Because of Cole, I was the walking dead. It was only a matter of time before their attacks worsened. I had to escape before I fell right into their trap.

Preston sneered at me, running his hands down his wet arms to create some warmth. "You might as well run while you can," he said through chattering teeth. "We'll even give you a head start."

Cole

I dropped into the armchair beside the couch and pounded the water bottle in my hand. Hunter glared at me out of the corner of his eye. He kicked his foot up on the coffee table and folded his arms over his chest.

"We crossed the line," Hunter said with his eyes on the wall. "You need to tell the other cadets to leave Grace alone. She learned her lesson. This was enough."

"I agree," Brax chimed, "She doesn't deserve this."

"This isn't about what she deserves. She has to earn her place just like everyone else."

"C'mon, Cole." Hunter leaned forward, his elbows rested on his thighs. "You're not doing all this shit for fun. Even you're not that sick."

"You went all Zero Dark Thirty on everyone because of Julian," Brax said.

I narrowed my eyes at him. "Watch it."

He smirked. "It's true. You hate how close he's getting to Grace. By pushing her away, you gave him an advantage. I don't blame him. I'd do the same thing if I were him."

"She has to go," I said to no one in particular, ignoring Brax's comments. "I spoke with my dad earlier. The Lucaya Group knows The Devil's Knights have Grace. They're looking for her."

Like Hunter and me, Brax had sworn an oath to protect Grace. She didn't know how corrupt and fucked up our world was. No clue she wasn't really Grace Hale, but someone else entirely. A girl that would have grown up to be a monster if her biological father had raised her instead of John Hale.

"The Founders Society is under fire, which means all of us are in danger."

"They don't know Grace is at the academy," Brax said.

"No." I steepled my hands on my thighs, my gaze flicking between them. "But it won't be long before someone traces her movements back to us."

"We can leave the academy," Hunter suggested. "Use one of the Knights' safe houses temporarily until we know who's coming for Grace."

"The Knights have a lead on the identities of the highest-ranking members of The Lucaya Group. Grace's biological father is one of them. He might even be their leader."

My dad started as a Knight, just like me, and after I was Knighted, he ascended to The Founders Society.

The Founders Society included the family members of the Founding Fathers of the United States. All of us had to prove our lineage. Hunter, Brax, and I could all trace our roots to one of the forefathers.

Brax stared at me, shocked. "Are you sure her dad is the leader?"

"It's a rumor." I shrugged. "Who knows if it's true."

"Her dad is one scary motherfucker." Hunter scrubbed a hand across his jaw. "If he ever gets his hands on her..."

"It will never happen," I assured him, though my voice lacked confidence. "She has us."

"Then start fucking acting like it," Hunter yelled, nostrils flared. "Call off the other cadets before something happens to her. Lay down Marshall Law. No one will go near her for the rest of the school year. You're drawing too much attention to her."

"My dad put his foot in his mouth when he announced Grace was the test case for the female cadet program. It would have been one thing to hide her on campus. But it's another to let her live among us, throwing the new cadet program in everyone's face. For all we know, there are students at this school working with The Lucaya Group."

"Not a chance," Hunter challenged. "The Founders vet everyone who steps foot onto this campus."

"Real monsters don't hide in the dark," I pointed out. "Grace's dad was a KGB agent before he went rogue. He knows how to manipulate people to get what he wants. That's how he tricked Grace's mother. He even fooled the Founders."

"And he's been in hiding ever since," Brax commented.

When Grace was seven years old, the Founders exposed her biological father as a fraud. He'd been living in the United States under a fake name, pretending to be a new money tech entrepreneur when he met Grace's mom. Rich and beautiful, Grace's mother passed her good looks and money to her daughter.

Grace's dad used her mom to get to the Founders, but his plan backfired. The Founders discovered his past. Then her dad attempted to kill her mother, who threw herself in front of Grace to save her. Somehow, Grace had no recollection of her past. Either the Founders had somehow erased her memories, or they were so painful her brain suppressed them.

"Chasing Grace from campus is the wrong move," Hunter said, leveling me with a cruel stare. "After last night, she'll do something stupid like hop the back fence. And she won't figure out until she's on the road that there's no civilization for thirty miles. Is that really a good plan, Cole? Let her wander through the wilderness until someone kidnaps her. Maybe someone will rape and murder her, too." Jaw clenched, he shot up from the couch. "Is this really what you think is best for her?"

I rose to my feet. "What do suggest, Hunter? Since you're so fucking smart, how would you handle the situation?"

"We should leave school. Grab Grace and get the fuck out of here." Hunter stuffed his hands into his pockets, meeting my gaze. "If we leave now, we can go with a plan."

"I like this idea," Brax confirmed.

"My dad wants us to wait a little while longer and see how this plays out."

"If you would publicly claim her, the cadets would settle down and leave her alone."

"Why don't *you* claim her?" I countered. "If it's so important to you."

"Because the cadets respect Marshall Law," Hunter fired back. "They follow *your* lead. So lead them and stop acting like a dickhead."

"Fine."

I turned to walk away, and Hunter grabbed my elbow. "She needs us, Cole. We've been friends for a long time. That's why I go along with most of your plans." He tipped his head toward Brax. "The three of us are brothers. But this is one thing neither of us agrees with you about. You need to fix this with Grace. Make it right before you get her killed."

Before I could answer, the door flew open. Julian—that lying prick—stood in the entryway with an angry snarl on his lips. He slammed the door and crossed the room with his hands balled into fists at his sides.

I threw out my hand. "Take another step, and I'll fucking end you."

"Go fuck yourself, Marshall," Julian said with venom in his tone. "I'm sick of your stupid games."

"I don't care who your family bribed to get you into this school. But I don't trust your lying ass. I will find out who you really are, and when I do, Grace will know. So you better stay away from her."

Standing a few feet from me, Julian moved his hands to hips, his expression unreadable. He didn't seem phased by my threat. My private investigator still hadn't uncovered the mystery behind the murder at Blackwell Military Academy. I hadn't raised the issued with the Founders because my dad wouldn't let me.

The old man insisted Julian was telling the truth and to leave things alone. He swore he had nothing to do with the decision to move Julian into my room. But he let him keep his rank, which still pissed me off. I'd worked my ass off to get my position, and he just waltzed in here without having to do a fucking thing.

Julian pointed his finger at me. "You better leave Grace alone."

"Or what?" I laughed in his face. "What power do you have here?"

He pressed his lips together.

"None. My point exactly. Grace is my business. So stay the fuck out of it."

"Don't worry about Grace," Hunter cut in. "She has everything she needs right here."

"If that were true, you assholes wouldn't be putting her through hell. She says you used to be her friends. Could have fooled me."

"Like I said, Grace is not your business."

Julian shook his head, realizing this conversation was going nowhere, and headed into his room without another word.

"He's too close to Grace," Brax said. "You need to do the right thing and take Grace off the market. Lay your claim to her in front of the cadets."

I never wanted to force Grace into anything. I'd always given her a choice.

"We'll move her into our apartment," I told my friends.

Brax nodded, while Hunter plastered a big ass smile on his face.

Grace

After classes ended for the day, I reported for cadet training. We started each session in formation while the staff officers shouted orders. Then, they went down the line inspecting our PT clothes—navy shorts with the gold YMA logo and a matching T-shirt. They printed PLEBE on the backs of our shirts, so everyone knew we were not cadets if they saw us on campus.

Most of the guys in my cadet class got high-fives and cheerful words of encouragement. But not me. When the cadets saw me, some of them spit at me. Others yelled obscenities and told me to leave before they forced me out.

They relegated those who failed to complete the final course on the first day to the C Squad. That was a badge of dishonor, a stain on your reputation. I was on B Squad with everyone who finished in over four minutes. The elite was in A Squad and rubbed their completion times in our faces.

No one had come close to Cole's record-breaking time. When he wasn't busy with platoon commander duties, he stopped by our training sessions to bullshit with the staff. He knew everyone who worked at the school. I figured Cole showed up to observe me, to see if I would fall flat on my face. Everyone had underestimated me. The cadets had even tried to stop me from completing the tasks on time.

They could push me down.

But I would always get up.

My dad raised a fighter.

I took one last look at Cole, who stood off to the side, his arms crossed over his chest. He leaned over to whisper to the drill sergeant beside him and nodded as he glanced at me. The drill sergeant gave the final order to the group. After we broke away from the pack, we entered the woods. Each squad had to complete a different obstacle course by the end of the eight-week training.

Mathis and Thompson kept pace with me, shooting daggers at me. The sun beat down on my back. For fall, it was hotter than usual. Even with the breeze floating off the water, sweat trickled down my skin.

Hauling ass past my teammates, who only looked out for themselves, I kept my head high and focused on my time. I wasn't dumb enough to think my squad had my back. As expected, Swanson came up on my right, cutting through the underbrush to reach me. He hated me with a passion and wanted me gone from the start.

So I veered off the path, breaking away from the trees marked with red arrows.

He didn't take the bait and stayed on the path. I continued running in the opposite direction, hoping to lose a few of them before I made my way back to the hiking trail. But the farther I trekked, the more uncertainty clouded my judgment. I thought I knew the woods well enough to retrace my steps.

Pushing down the fear creeping up my spine, I forced myself to run faster, hoping I could cut through the trails and meet the cadets in the middle. We hadn't run this course before, so I wasn't sure what to expect. Would we have another cargo net climb? Maybe tires or ropes? Each day differed from the next.

Finally, I found my way back and started making headway. Based on the tree markers, I was only a minute or two behind the other cadets. They would harass me for being the weak link, but it beat getting my head bashed in by these psychos. My squad was just as unpredictable as the cadets in my platoon.

I bolted down the dirt path and came to a screeching halt when I spotted a man by the tree marker. He leaned against the bark, his dark hair partially covered by a bandana, black paint smeared on his face, making it impossible to distinguish him from the others. A wicked smile turned up the corners of his mouth when our eyes met.

Was he waiting for me?

My heart slammed into my chest with the force of a truck. Hands balled into fists at my sides, I prepared myself for a fight. He was at least six feet tall and solid muscle. While he had weight and height over me, I was small and fast. Dad had showed me how to use my disadvantages to my advantage.

Trust your instincts, Grace.

When in doubt, I always heard my dad's voice. He didn't need to be with me to help guide the way. The man was about a hundred feet away. I didn't have any weapons, only my smarts and my fists. So that would have to do.

Taking off in the opposite direction, I plowed through the underbrush, hauling ass toward the school. I didn't bother to glance over my shoulder, even when I heard him running after me.

A single second mattered.

Never give your opponent an advantage.

As I darted through the woods, sweat slid down my forehead and into my eyes. I blinked away the sweat. The soles of my boots pounded the dirt that squished beneath my feet. My limbs burned from exhaustion, begging for me to slow down. But that was impossible. I turned at the end of the path, and a knife whizzed past my head and slammed into the tree.

Holy shit!

The psychopath threw another knife, this one grazing my earlobe. A searing hot pain coursed over me, and blood dripped down my neck. Through the trees, I could see the outline of the school from a distance. Relief washed over me, but it was too early to celebrate.

When I darted out of the woods like a bat out of hell, I didn't stop when the drill sergeant ordered me to halt.

Fuck that shit.

I didn't even look in his direction or check behind me. Because if that lunatic were still hunting me like an animal, he would have to go through trained officers to get to me. So I ran as fast as my feet would allow, undeterred by the cadets who tried to get in my way across campus. I could hardly breathe by the time I pulled open the door to Bryant Hall and ran upstairs to the second floor.

Without even thinking, I rushed down the hall and banged on the door to room 207. I hated to ask for their help, but I knew I needed it. Brax swung open the door, shirtless with mesh basketball shorts hanging low from his narrow hips. He wasn't as muscular as Cole and Hunter, but he was solid and covered in tattoos.

I bent forward to catch my breath and choked out, "I think someone tried to kill me."

Brax gripped my bicep and led me into the apartment, helping me onto the couch. He plopped down beside me and studied my face. "Tell me what happened, Grace."

I rested my palms on my knees for support. My thoughts were a scattered mess. What the hell just happened out there? Brax waved his hand in front of my eyes when I didn't respond.

He blew out a deep breath, then removed his cell phone from his pocket. "Hunter," Brax shouted as his fingers slid across the keypad. He typed a quick message to Cole and dropped his phone on the coffee table in front of us. "Get your ass out here. We have an emergency."

Hunter popped his head out of his bedroom on the left side of the apartment. He stepped into the room in a pair of super-tight black boxer briefs that hugged his best assets perfectly.

Why was he always in his underwear?

Hunter surveyed my appearance with concern. "What's wrong, Grace?"

Brax slid across the couch and tilted my head to the side. "Why are you bleeding?"

"Someone chased me through the woods and threw knives at my head."

"What?" Hunter said in disbelief and moved to the other side of me. He leaned over me and inspected my bleeding ear, and then he headed into the kitchen to grab a wet rag. Dropping to the couch beside me, Hunter held the cloth to my ear to stop the bleeding. "Start from the beginning. Don't leave out any details."

I rehashed the events of the afternoon, and by the

time I finished, the front door flew open. Cole's gaze found mine, intense and terrifying. He slammed the door and lowered to his knees on the floor in front of me. No one spoke a single word as he cupped the side of my face.

His jaw clenched. "Did you get a good look at him?"

I shook my head. "He had paint on his face."

He set his hand on my knee and tapped his fingers. "What did he look like?"

"Tall, probably around your height. Muscular with dark hair."

"Any tattoos or anything that stood out about him?"

"No. He wore black cammies, a black bandana, and black face paint. A cadet in Squad B fucked with me. So I took a shortcut, thinking I could make it back to the trail before I lost my team. And then I ran into him."

Hunter gripped my shoulder. "Did he say anything?"

"No. But he was waiting for me."

"Which cadet fucked with you on the main path?" Brax asked.

"Rick Swanson."

Hunter looked at Brax. "Go find Swanson."

Brax rubbed my back in a soothing, gentle motion that comforted me. I didn't know him as well as Cole and Hunter, but he'd always seemed like a decent guy. He shot up from the couch and left the apartment without further instruction.

Cole took Brax's place beside me and pulled me into his arms. He rested his chin on top of my head and hugged me. Hunter slid across the leather and lifted my legs onto his lap. While Cole stroked his fingers through my messy hair, Hunter massaged my calves. After all of the torture at the academy, they were finally treating me like I was theirs again.

It felt like old times.

"He wasn't a cadet, was he?"

Hunter shook his head.

"No," Cole agreed. "Doesn't sound like one."

I sat up and slipped out of Cole's arms, leaning my back against the cushions between them.

"From now on, you need to stay with us," Hunter said.

Cole agreed with him.

"I enjoy living by myself."

Cole's hand inched up my thigh, and now I was all too aware of his hard body pressed against mine. "Stay with us. You'll be safer here."

"I wouldn't have my own room."

"You can take turns spending the night in our beds." Hunter waggled his eyebrows, a smirk in place. "What do you say, baby girl?"

"Oh, so now I'm your baby girl again?" I sighed.

"How do you two expect me to erase the past from my brain? I can't trust either of you."

"When it comes to your life," Cole said in a severe tone, "there's nothing I take more seriously."

He flipped over my hand and traced an infinity symbol on my palm with his index finger. The sudden motion sucked the air from my lungs. For a moment, I thought about my dad and the last time we were together. He did this every time he left because this was our version of always and forever.

I peeked up at Cole, who was already looking down at me with sad blue eyes. "Why did you push me away after your mom died?"

"Because I thought I was doing the right thing. I was trying to protect you. But pushing you away only put you in more danger."

"For the record," Hunter cut in, "I didn't want to let you go. That was Cole's idea."

"Dickhead," Cole groaned. "Shut your fucking mouth."

Hunter rolled his big shoulders and gave his best friend a lopsided grin. "It's true." His fingers inched up my inner thigh. "I call dibs on your first night in the apartment."

I scoffed at his presumption. "Who says I'm going to live here with you?"

"It's not up for debate," Cole said with authority. "I'm not taking any more chances with your life."

"I'll think about it."

"No thinking." Cole hooked his arm around me and kissed my forehead. "You're mine, brat."

I had dreamed of hearing those words for too long. As I relaxed in his arms, I drank in his manly scent and basked in the feeling of my cadets.

"Won't the board deny my room change? Your dad put me in the officer's quarters because of the same-sex rules."

"I don't care about the fucking board," Cole shot back. "If they have a problem with it, they can take it up with me. You're not going anywhere."

"I don't love your mood swings."

"Get used to them." Cole's lips brushed my cheek. "You're stuck with me, brat."

Cole

While Grace was in the shower, Brax stormed into the apartment, dragging Swanson by his collar. He dropped his sorry ass on the floor at my feet.

I reached down and wrapped my hand around his throat. "Who are you working with?"

His eyes widened. "I'm not working with anyone. I don't know what you're talking about."

"You pushed Grace Hale off the path, and someone tried to kill her. Who ordered you to do it?"

"I… I don't," he stammered, ready to piss himself. "I don't know their names. They're seniors, I think."

Brax yanked Swanson's head back, fisting his hair. "You better give us a name and say it fast."

"I don't know his name."

"Bullshit," I snapped. "Our last names are on our uniforms. Give me a fucking name. Now!"

"Carter," he choked out.

"Preston Carter?"

He nodded. "Please don't tell him I told."

"That motherfucker. What did he tell you to do?"

"He gave me five hundred dollars to scare her. None of the cadets want her at YMA."

Preston Carter didn't have connections to The Lucaya Group. His family was squeaky clean. They didn't even have parking tickets, let alone ties to a deadly criminal organization.

"Get out." I flung my hand at the door. "Go before I string you up in the courtyard by your balls."

Swanson scrambled to his feet, tripping over his boots. He slammed headfirst into the door, a nervous mess as he reached for the doorknob and made his escape.

Eyes on the door, Hunter shook his head and laughed. "Well, I think it's safe to say he didn't try to kill Grace."

Brax smirked. "That's for damn sure. How did he even get on B Squad? He has zero hand-eye coordination."

"Because he cheats," Grace said, drawing our attention to her.

She stood outside the bathroom door, a towel wrapped around her curves, teasing me with those pouty pink lips. When she arrived at the apartment, she had dirt on her clothes and blood dripping down her neck. But now, she looked like the same pretty doll I became obsessed with ten years ago. Now that she was living under my roof, I wasn't letting her out of my sight.

Brax's mouth hung open as he stared at Grace. Hunter was only wearing black boxer briefs, so it wasn't hard to miss his growing bulge.

I raised my hand and beckoned her with my finger. "Come here, Grace."

She gave me an apprehensive look, then crossed the room, standing at the center of our group. Brax was never part of the equation before. But if she wanted him, I would never deny her. I already knew Brax was dying to get his hands on our girl.

Her eyes darted between us before settling on me. "What did Swanson say?"

"Preston paid him to get rid of you," I told her. "But he wasn't the person who tried to kill you."

She narrowed her eyes at me. "Why would someone want to kill me over losing points for the Command Cup?"

"I don't think he was a student."

Grace pressed her lips together and surveyed me with suspicion. "So Swanson forcing me off the path was a happy accident for someone else to attack me?"

I nodded. "Seems that way. From now on, you're not leaving this apartment without one of us."

"What about Julian?"

I shook my head. "He's not one of us."

She stood straight and flicked her long, wet hair over her shoulder. "I'm not giving him up just because I'm moving in with you. He's my friend, too."

"I wanna be your friend," Brax said with a lazy smile.

Grace laughed.

"Grace's safety is our number one priority." I aimed a warning glare at Brax. "This is not the time to be thinking with your dick."

He snickered. "Who said anything about sex?"

"Okay, boys," Grace interjected. "No need to fight over me. We have more important things to think about right now. Like figuring out who wants to kill me."

"That's a long list," I told her.

Brax removed his cell phone from his pocket. "I'll get started with the security feeds on campus."

"I'll talk to campus security and see if they've had any suspicious visitors today," Hunter offered before walking toward his bedroom.

Grace tilted her head back and gave me a hopeful look. "I hope you guys find that bastard. He could have killed me."

"We will," I promised. "We won't let them touch you."

She raised an eyebrow. "Them?"

Shit.

"I mean him. We'll find him."

I meant *them*.

After The Lucaya Group murdered my mother and then posed her to look like she committed suicide,

I panicked and shut out Grace. I'd left her unprotected, vulnerable, even made her a target for the cadets. She deserved better than me. The Founders would never approve of our relationship, and they especially wouldn't want us sharing her.

Grace stood on her tippy toes and pressed a kiss to my lips. I hooked my arm around her back and carried her to the kitchen island. I set her on the marble, making room for myself between her thighs. Her towel fell open, revealing her gorgeous body. I cupped her breast in my hand, and she whimpered when I rolled my thumb over her nipple.

"Cole, I'm still mad at you."

I dipped my head down and kissed her lips. "I'm sorry, Grace. I shouldn't have handled the situation the way I did."

"How are you going to make it up to me?"

"My little brat," I said before parting her lips with my tongue, holding the back of her head so I could deepen the kiss. "How do you want me to make it up to you?"

"Orgasms," she whispered. "Lots and lots of orgasms."

I smiled. "I can do that."

Grace unzipped my pants and whipped out my cock, giving me a few tentative strokes. I removed my blazer, shirt, and tie in a hurry.

She ran her hands down my chest and shoved my

pants and boxer briefs over my hips. "Get rid of these," she ordered.

"Yes, ma'am," I said with a wink.

After I stripped off my clothes, I guided my cock between her slick folds. She was always so wet for me. I remembered when we were teenagers, and every time I touched her, she moaned. It was like she couldn't control herself. A simple back massage or even a kiss had her soaked through her panties.

I gripped her hips and slammed into her, each time harder than the last. She loved when I was rough. Sex with Grace was therapeutic, like I could cleanse myself of all my wrongdoings with each orgasm I stole from her.

I spread her open, shoving my cock deeper and deeper, burying myself inside her. Her nails dug into my shoulders, tearing through my skin as she screamed my name, riding out her first orgasm. Grabbing her ass cheeks, I lifted her off the counter and took her harder, tearing screams from her mouth with each thrust. Grace's tits bounced as I fucked her.

"Harder, Cole," she whimpered, her entire body shaking through me, and I quickened my pace. She licked her lips as her eyes met mine. "I missed you."

"I missed you, too, brat."

Without breaking stride, my lips crashed against hers. I whispered how much I had missed her between kisses, fucking her so hard I hoped she would remember who owned her body.

Her eyes moved from mine to the far side of the room. Hunter leaned against the wall outside of his bedroom, still wearing his boxers and stroking his cock through the slit. That was how it started with us. He'd walked in on Grace and me, and she invited him to stay.

The fucker never left after that night.

Brax looked like he wasn't breathing as he stared at Grace's tits slapping against my chest. Unlike Hunter, he wasn't an animal. He was the type to observe, hunt, and then go in for the kill at the right moment, while Hunter had zero self-control.

"Hunter," Grace moaned. "You gonna come for me, big guy?"

He stroked his cock harder and licked his lips. "Yeah, baby. You going to come for us?"

"Uh-huh," she moaned, her nails sinking deeper into my skin.

"I can't believe I've been missing out on this," Brax said in a hushed tone, though his voice carried across the room.

"You've just ruined Brax," I told Grace, who was at the peak of her climax.

She tipped her head back and moaned each of our names as if Brax had been part of the group all along. Hunter came right after her. Brax just watched the scene play out, his cock tenting his pants. It wasn't much longer before I chased my high, desperate to lose myself in Grace.

I crashed on top of her. We kissed for a few seconds before I pulled out and kissed her again. Hunter moved to the kitchen island to wash the cum from his hand, his dick still hanging out of his boxer briefs. Brax seemed excited but also somewhat bewildered by the exchange between us.

"You're killing me, baby girl," Hunter groaned. "Break my heart, why don't you? You let Cole fuck you first." He shook his head, drying his hands with a kitchen towel. "He's been a bastard this whole time."

"I've always been nice to you," Brax chimed to earn brownie points. "What's a man gotta do to get some love around here?"

Grace laughed and didn't even bother to cover herself with the bath towel on the counter beneath her. "I'm taking turns sleeping in each of your beds. There's enough of me to go around."

Hunter gave her a victorious smile. "You're mine tonight."

I didn't protest since I got to fuck her first.

"What night do I sleep in Brax's bed?" Grace asked.

"You're with Hunter tonight," I confirmed. "Me tomorrow night. And Brax the night after that… if you want to sleep with him."

Grace took one look at him and licked her lips. "Okay. I'm good with that."

A loud bang drew our attention to the door. Julian stumbled inside, dressed in his uniform, a duffel slung over his shoulder. His eyes widened as he walked into the living room.

"I'm with Julian the night after Brax," Grace announced.

"What's going on here?" Julian lifted an eyebrow in question, slowly approaching the kitchen. "And why is everyone naked?"

"Orgy virgin," Hunter quipped.

"We didn't have an orgy," Grace shot back. "Cole fucked me. You jerked off. Brax just watched."

"I'm *not* okay with him," I said. "Archer isn't part of the rotation."

"It's non-negotiable." Grace grinned. "He's my friend, which makes him your friend now."

"Rotation for what?" Julian asked, confused as fuck.

"I'm moving in with all of you," Grace told him, with her legs spread wide and slick with our cum. "And since I don't have my own room, I'm taking turns sleeping with each of you."

Julian's eyes moved up and down her body. "Oh, yeah? Sign me up for that."

"That sounded creepy, dude." Hunter slapped

Julian on the back as he headed toward his room. "Might want to tone down the desperation."

I slid my fingers beneath Grace's chin. "Get dressed in uniform. It's almost time for dinner. The platoon commander can't be late."

Grace hopped down from the counter. "I need another shower."

Hunter raised his hand. "I got dibs on that."

"Dibs on what?" Julian asked.

"Who gets a turn with Grace in the shower."

Julian appraised Grace's naked body. "You're okay with this?"

She nodded.

"You want all four of us?"

The concept seemed foreign to Archer.

Grace's eyes swept over each of us. "Yes. All of you are my cadets."

He moved his hand to her hip and pulled her closer. "So, what are the rules?"

"Cole will make them," she said without hesitation because she knew me so well.

Hunter nodded in agreement. So did Brax.

Grace placed her palm on his chest. "You okay with that?"

I didn't like Archer, but if Grace wanted him, there wasn't much I could do about it. He came with the package... until I could prove he was a liar or get rid of him. Either way, he would not be a permanent fixture in our group.

Julian agreed to follow whatever rules I made, and then Grace kissed my enemy. So we were doing this, all five of us under one roof. This would not end well.

Grace

After agreeing to live with Cole and the guys, I dressed in my uniform and followed my platoon to the mess hall. My stomach twisted in knots from the incident in the woods.

Someone had tried to kill me.

He sought me out, hunted me like an animal. If my dad hadn't trained me for any situation, I probably would have been dead.

Cole and Hunter ordered the cadets to switch seats. As usual, Cole sat at the head of the table. Except now I was on his right and Hunter on his left. Julian was beside me with Brax on the other side of Hunter.

The sudden shift in the platoon garnered a lot of attention from the other tables. Of course, we had the eyes and ears of most of the cadets on an average day. But today, Cole and the guys were laying their claim to me publicly.

I felt like a queen with four sexy kings.

Throughout dinner, I thought about how I was one lucky girl. Sure, our relationship was unconventional and weird to outsiders, but we could make it work.

One girl. Four boyfriends. I was sure someone had done it before.

Julian placed his hand on my thigh under the table, and Cole's eyes narrowed. The tension between them sent a wave of electricity up my arms. He said he would learn to live with Julian as part of our unit, but he clearly would have rather killed him.

I patted Julian's hand. "He'll chill out eventually."

He snorted. "I wouldn't count on it."

Cole, Brax, and Hunter watched us.

"This will not work if you don't get along," I told them.

A few of the cadets to my right craned their ears to listen. Cole shook his head in warning, and I shut my mouth.

"Eat your food and mind your business," Cole told the cadets at our table, fisting his fork so tightly his knuckles drained of color.

Everyone resumed eating dinner in silence, eyes on their plates. I shoveled rice into my mouth, ignoring the sinful glances I got from my cadets. Their wicked looks set my skin on my fire, my body tingling with desire. After our sexual encounter earlier, I couldn't wait until it was my turn to sleep in each of their beds. I'd missed Cole and Hunter. And I was looking forward to getting to know Julian and Brax better.

After I finished my food, a loud moan echoed throughout the mess hall. I glanced around the room in search of the source. A woman moaned again, this time louder and followed by the heavy breathing of what sounded like not one but two men.

"Harder, Cole."

My mouth fell open at the sound of my voice, and heat spread across my cheeks.

"Oh, my God, Hunter," I whimpered. "Mmm…"

It sounded like the video we'd sent to Preston over the summer. And as I looked around the room, I spotted three flat-screen televisions hung on the wall. They usually played the news on an insanely low volume you couldn't even hear.

Today, it was the video of Cole and Hunter fucking me at the same time.

I hooked my arms around Cole's neck and rode his cock while Hunter fucked me from behind. Hunter wrapped his fingers around my throat, tilting my head back to kiss my lips. My skin burned with a mixture of desire and anger.

"What the fuck?" Cole shot up from his chair and pointed his finger at the TV. "Who's responsible for this?"

No one answered him.

Everyone whispered as I moaned and begged Cole and Hunter for more. Sandwiched between two sexy cadets, my breasts bounced in Cole's face. There wasn't much of us you couldn't see clearly on the screen. We did too good of a job filming that night.

I rose from the table in unison with the rest of my cadets.

"I'm gonna kill him." Hunter gritted his teeth. "That fucking bastard."

I followed his line of sight down the table. Preston laughed so hard he clutched his chest. As usual, Grayson and Rhys went along with his bullshit. The entire room burst into an uproar. Some of them laughed and pointed at me. Others just stared at the video like it was normal to watch porn together. I noticed a few guys reach under the table to fix themselves.

Hello, awkward.

Half the room hated me, and the other half wanted to fuck me.

Julian clutched my shoulder. "It's okay, Grace. Let us deal with them."

"No." I grabbed a butter knife from the table. "He's mine."

Before my cadets could stop me, I raced toward Preston and his stupid fucking friends, who wouldn't stop moaning as I approached them.

"Jesus, Hale," one boy at our table groaned, licking his lips. "Ride my cock like that."

"I'm in room 212," another guy said.

"Not a fucking chance," I snapped.

Whore, slut, skank, barracks bunny, and every word imaginable fell from the lips of my classmates. I ignored their taunts and focused on my ex-boyfriend, who was dead fucking meat.

Gripping the knife to steady my nerves, it made indentations in my palm. "Turn off the video," I yelled at Preston. "Now!"

"No can do, G.I. Barbie." An evil grin tugged at the corners of his mouth. "You think you're so tough. What do you think they'll do to you now that they've seen you taking two cocks at the same time?"

I gritted my teeth. "Jealous it's not yours?"

"Nah, babe." Preston grabbed his crotch and smirked. "You couldn't handle my cock. That's why I replaced you with someone else."

"Please." I tilted my head back and laughed like a maniac. "Like I could even find your tiny dick. You must tire of women asking, 'Is it in yet?'"

The table roared with laughter.

"She's joking," Preston said in his defense.

My moans stopped. And when I peeked over my shoulder, Cole, Hunter, and Brax had yanked the plugs from the wall on each of the televisions.

"No, I'm not," I challenged, hovering over his chair, the knife burning my palm. "I couldn't find your dick with a magnifying glass and a compass."

People laughed.

Preston thought he could humiliate me so I would leave the school. Sure, I was embarrassed beyond belief, but I wasn't going anywhere. Most of the guys at this school had already undressed me with their eyes.

Our entire platoon had seen me wet, naked, and wrapped in paper towels because of the shower incident. There wasn't much they hadn't looked at yet. And now they knew the exact sounds I made when two cadets fucked me and how I looked when they did.

"You're going to die a slow, painful death," Preston grunted. "Just like your father."

I jumped onto Preston's lap and pressed the knife to his throat. Not like a butter knife would hurt him. Just the threat alone, and the way he squirmed beneath me, made me instantly feel better.

"Wanna say that again, you sick fuck?" I shoved my fingers through his hair and tugged hard. "I won't think twice about letting my hand slip."

He laughed, spit hitting my chin. "You think you'll survive cadet training. Guess again. You're on everyone's radar now."

"You had your chance," Rhys said to me. "You could have been ours."

"She always chooses losers," Preston said with a sneer. "Besides, you don't want Marshall and Banks's sloppy seconds. Her pussy would probably swallow your dick whole."

I pressed harder and sliced into his neck.

"Crazy bitch," he growled, attempting to shove me off his lap. "You're going to pay for that, little slut."

"Call me whatever you want," I breathed in his face. "If you think a sex tape is going to shame me, you've got another thing coming. I'm not leaving the academy. You tried to kill me earlier. Nice try, but it's going to take a lot more to get rid of me."

"I didn't try to kill you. If I wanted you dead, you wouldn't be here."

I slid off his lap and dropped the knife onto the table. "Then who did?"

He rolled his shoulders. "Take your pick, Hale. Everyone here is out for your blood."

A warm body pressed against my back, strong arms wrapped around me. Julian pushed me behind him, then leaned down to grip the collar of Preston's shirt. "You piece of shit," he yelled in his face before punching him in the nose.

Preston's head turned to the side from the sheer force of the hit. He spit at Julian and missed his face by a few inches. "You're done at YMA, Archer."

I tugged on Julian's blazer. "He's not worth it. Let's get out of here."

Preston scrubbed a hand across his jaw. "How many men does it take to satisfy you, little whore?"

"Four," I said with no shame.

Preston tilted his head to the side and looked at Cole, Hunter, and Brax, who were issuing commands to our platoon. Then his eyes were on Julian and me. He shook his head, disgusted by my comment.

I slipped my fingers between Julian's and turned my back on Preston. "C'mon, let's go."

On our way across the room, I stopped to tell Cole and the guys we were going outside to get some air. They couldn't leave since they were in charge of those around us. I also didn't want them taking shots at the other cadets because it would jeopardize their positions at the academy.

Cole told us to take a lap and then meet them at the apartment. We darted through the halls until we were out the front door and walking toward Walker Pass. Julian's grip tightened on my hand, soothing the nerves shooting throughout my body.

"I can't believe he did that," I said as we passed the massive water fountain at the center of the square. "Preston's had the video since the summer. Why show it now?"

"To get rid of you."

"Do you think he had anything to do with the man who chased me through the woods?"

Julian shrugged. "I don't know. But I'll find out."

When we approached the woods, I peeked up at him. The thought of entering the woods after the incident earlier chilled me to the bone.

"Where are we going?"

Eyes on the path ahead, he pressed his lips together. "The beach."

He was reticent once we entered the woods, swatting at the underbrush in our way. When his long fingers held mine with rough possession, a chill rushed down my arms, dotting my skin. The usual hoots and howls rolled across the quiet terrain. But it was the silence between us that freaked me out.

Something was wrong.

"Julian, slow down." I halted, forcing him to stop. "What's the rush?"

He stared down at me, barely breathing, expressionless as his eyes met mine. "We don't have time." Then he yanked my hand, leading me down the path with a purpose.

"Time for what?" I shouted, scratching my nails down his arm. "What is wrong with you, Julian? You're scaring me. Stop it."

"I'm sorry, Grace." He lifted me in his arms and carried me the rest of the way to the beach. "I didn't want to do this."

I rolled back and forth, trying to break his hold on me. "Julian, put me down. You're acting like a lunatic."

"I want you to know I didn't have a choice."

"A choice in what?"

We moved toward the boat at the edge of the water.

"Julian, please." I punched him in the arm. "Put me down. What are you doing?"

"I wish I didn't have to do this."

A dark-haired man with a beard stood on the boat,

his foot propped up on a bench. He was probably somewhere close to sixty. Two other men dressed in all black stepped off the boat. They looked like hired thugs, dangerous and covered in dark ink.

"You did well," the man on the boat told Julian with an evil grin plastered on his face. "The boss has waited a long time to see his daughter."

The boss?

Daughter?

If they were talking about me, they had the wrong girl. My dad was six feet under. I'd never seen this man before, and his voice didn't sound the least bit recognizable. He had a Russian accent.

I scratched Julian's neck until I drew blood, and he hissed as crimson slid down his skin. "Please, Julian. Don't do this. Whatever they offered you, Cole will give you ten times the amount."

"This isn't about money." Julian lowered me to the sand. "Where is my sister?"

Sister? What the hell is going on?

"You said she would be here for the exchange," Julian added. "We made a deal. I upheld my end of the bargain."

"She's at the island." He pointed into the expanse of the ocean. "Bring the girl. We'll make the exchange there."

Julian's stance shifted. Then he pushed me behind

him. "That wasn't the deal, Sergei. My sister for Viktor's daughter."

He shook his head. "Change of plans."

"Run," Julian whispered, shoving his palm into my stomach.

Because I wasn't an idiot, I did as he instructed and hauled ass across the sand toward the woods. A gunshot fired behind me. Loud grunts penetrated the air, then another shot fired. Julian was probably dead, but I didn't have time to care. That bastard was going to trade me for his sister.

Cole

I paced across the living room, waiting for Julian and Grace to return. They walked out of the mess hall during dinner and then disappeared. Grace wasn't in her old room, and no one on the floor had seen her.

I checked to see if she'd packed her shit, but nothing had changed. John Hale's dog tags sat on her dresser, something she would never leave behind.

"Sit down," Hunter said. "You're annoying the shit out of me."

I stopped moving for a second and glanced down at him. He laid across the couch with a contraband cell phone in his hand.

Brax was asleep on the other couch, with his head turned to the side, hair covering his eyes. He snored softly, his drawing tablet cradled against his chest. A picture of Grace dressed in navy blue cammies and a matching bra was on the screen. I noticed he'd been drawing her a lot lately.

"Julian did something to her," I said.

"We don't know for sure." Hunter sat up and dropped the cell phone on the coffee table. "She's probably blowing off steam somewhere. Preston destroyed her today."

After searching the campus, there was no sight of them. So we went back to our apartment. My dad promised to find her and report back when he had new information. Grace and Julian had to be somewhere on campus. They could not have gone far. Still, I didn't trust him, especially not with Grace.

"We should have gone after her," I said. "Instead, we let her walk away with a stranger."

Someone knocked on the door. I looked up at the clock on the wall in the kitchen. It was well after midnight. Brax rubbed the sleep from his eyes and peeked up at me. His tablet fell out of his hand and onto the couch.

"Get up," I told him before I raced across the room and pulled open the door. "Dad," I breathed, surprised to see him standing in the hallway in plain clothes. "Please tell me you have a lead on Grace."

The commandant blew out a deep breath. His eyes were red-rimmed as if he hadn't slept in days. He looked like shit, not even in his uniform, which was out of character for him. "Grace left the campus," my dad said as if he still couldn't believe it, running a hand through his dark hair.

My heart sank into my stomach. "How did she get past the guards?"

"She boarded a boat." He stepped into the apartment and closed the door, shaking his head. "The Founders vetted Julian Archer. I don't understand how they missed this."

"Dad, what arc you saying?"

"We believe Julian is working with The Lucaya Group."

Hunter shot up from the couch. "You let him sleep under our roof without digging into his past?"

"We checked into him," Dad said. "There wasn't anything suspicious in his past."

"He killed someone at his last school." I threw my hands in the air. "I even printed the article for you, and you refused to take me seriously."

"The blog wasn't credible. I spoke with the Commandant of Blackwell Military Academy. He never believed Julian had anything to do with the murder."

"Someone died on his watch," I pointed out.

"They questioned Julian because he was the victim's roommate. The evidence showed Julian was across campus at the time of death. So he couldn't have killed the cadet."

"If he's working with The Lucaya Group, he's a trained killer. He only wanted the commandant to think he was somewhere else."

Dad dropped into the armchair beside the couch. "I rechecked the security footage before I left my office.

There are blank spots in the videos. Not just today but on other days."

"Which days?"

"The first weekend back at the academy. Saturday night."

"The night of the bonfire," Brax muttered.

Dad nodded. "From 2200 hours to 2245 hours, there's static on all the feeds. That late at night, the guards must not have been paying attention because the time jumps forty-five minutes in a flash."

He knew about everything that happened on campus, even our extracurriculars. He was a hard ass during the school week, but he didn't mind if we partied, as long as we didn't draw attention to ourselves.

Brax leaned forward, cupping his knees with his hands, his focus on my dad. "Julian went missing that night. Grace said someone chased her through the woods."

"Yeah," Hunter chimed. "We heard her screaming and followed her."

"Archer showed up a few minutes later," I added. "He acted as if nothing had happened, said he went back to the dorms."

"I didn't see him on the cameras," Dad confirmed.

I sat on the couch beside my dad. "I tried telling everyone he was full of shit. No one would listen to me."

Hunter crossed the living room and pushed open Julian's bedroom door. He emerged with a MacBook Air and plopped down on the couch beside me, flipping open the laptop. Hunter's fingers raced across the keys. He entered several passwords and sighed each time an error message popped up on the screen.

I leaned my elbow on the arm of the couch and looked at my dad. "Next time, maybe you'll listen to me."

Dad bit his lip. "If there is another time."

My heart beat so fast I struggled to speak. "How do we get her back?"

"Drake Battle and Marcello Salvatore are working on tracking her. The dog tags I gave her don't belong to John Hale. They have a tracking chip in them."

"She left them in her room," Hunter said as he set the laptop on the table. "Grace wasn't planning to leave with Julian."

"This is Preston's fault," I said with irritation in my tone. "If he hadn't made Grace look like a whore in front of the entire school, she wouldn't have left the mess hall with Archer."

"About the video." Dad's jaw clenched. "The Founders are now aware of it. What were you thinking, Cole? You had one job—to protect Grace—not fuck her." Then his eyes moved to Hunter. "And you? She's not some whore for you to pass around for your entertainment."

"I know how it looks," Hunter said in his defense, "but it's not what you think."

"Explain yourself," Dad ordered.

"We share Grace," Hunter said as if it were normal to share a woman with your best friend.

His eyes narrowed at me. "The three of you are in a relationship?"

I shook my head. "No, I'm not with Hunter. It's about Grace."

Dad ran a hand across the stubble on his jaw. "I don't understand you, Cole. What would possess the three of you to do something like that? I raised you better."

"Because we care about her," Hunter interjected. "It's not just sex."

My dad's gaze moved to me. "Is that true?"

I nodded.

"You have known from the day you met Grace that she's off-limits. The Founders trusted us to keep her safe."

"She was safe," I fired back. "You saw the video. Did Grace look like we forced her?"

"No," he muttered, his eyes on the floor. "But it doesn't give you the right to defile the granddaughter of The Founders Society's Grand Master."

Hunter typed feverishly, trying one password after another until he raised his arms, victorious. "I'm in."

I scooted across the leather couch until our thighs

touched, eyes on the screen as Hunter flipped through the folders on Julian's computer. Dad stood over us. Brax was on Hunter's right side, invading his space. We sat in silence as Hunter opened each folder, slowly revealing the deceit of our new roommate.

Grace was fucking gone.

Archer stole her from us.

My eyes burned, but the tears would never slide down my cheeks. I didn't cry, at least not like a normal person. I could feel the pain behind my eyes as if the tears wanted to spill from them, and then nothing would happen.

It was fucking weird.

I was seriously fucked-up.

Years of forcing down my feelings, being told that real men don't cry, had fucked with my emotions.

Julian had dozens of bank statements in one folder, each with deposits of over one hundred thousand dollars. Another folder contained pictures of Grace sleeping. In some, she wore Julian's T-shirt and black panties. Red-hot rage burned my skin at the sight of him touching her, kissing her, all of it caught on camera. The bastard filmed Grace without her knowing about it.

Hunter clicked on a video. From the thumbnail alone, I knew what we were about to watch and clenched my jaw. Grace was on top of Julian, grinding against him, still fully clothed.

"Turn it off," Dad said, unable to look at the video, and then aimed his hateful gaze at me. "How did you let this happen, Cole?"

"I'm not her keeper."

"You *are* her personal Knight. All three of you are in charge of Grace's safety. You fucked up your mission because you're thinking with the wrong head."

"No, we fucked up because you let the board put an outsider in our apartment. *You* allowed Archer to infiltrate our ranks."

Dad shook his head. "It was a mistake. Nothing appeared out of the ordinary with Julian Archer. His father is an oil tycoon, a respected businessman. I had no reason to believe he was working with The Lucaya Group."

Hunter scrolled through Julian's browser history, most of which was porn. His search yielded little, not until he found a hidden folder on the hard drive. He clicked on a folder titled *Movements*. There were complete reports about the whereabouts of influential members of The Devil's Knights and The Founders Society.

Julian had dozens of files on each of the Founding Families. He even had a folder on The Serpents. No one knew the identities of The Serpent Society. They were almost as mythical as their code names—Hades, Charon, Morpheus, and Lethe. And yet, Julian had images of each group member, along with their real names and past indiscretions.

Inside the Movements folder, Hunter clicked on one titled *Katarina Romanov Adams*, Grace's real name. Her biological grandfather ran the oldest and largest bank in the world, which placed a target on his back. The old man had more enemies than all of us combined. No one liked bankers, especially not Fitzgerald Archibald Adams IV. Grace was also related to Bastian Salvatore. She had a whole other life she didn't know about.

It was safer for us to place Grace with John Hale. This way, she didn't live in one city for too long. For years, it kept her out of harm's way while allowing her to travel the world. The plan was solid until The Lucaya Group murdered John.

"Open it," my dad ordered.

Hunter double-clicked on the folder and got a message that prompted him for a password. Again, he entered the same combination that opened the computer. But this time, a message displayed he had two more attempts.

"Be careful," Dad warned. "Whatever's in that folder could lead us to Grace."

Hunter dug his teeth into his lip. "Sure, no pressure. Only Grace's life on the line."

After two more attempts, the screen flashed red and kicked Hunter back to the home screen. Again, it prompted him for a password, and this time, the one he used didn't work. He tried a few more times with no success.

The unmistakable sound of the door handle jiggling snapped my attention toward the entrance. I jumped to my feet with Hunter and my dad at my side. Brax moved around the coffee table and stood on my left, his arms folded across his chest as the door swung open.

A beat-up-looking Julian stepped into the living room. His cadet uniform was in tatters, blood running down his bruised face. "Let me explain."

I slammed my fist into the wall on the side of his head. "Where the fuck is she?"

Julian raised his hands in surrender. "Just give me a chance. I know how to find her, but I need your help."

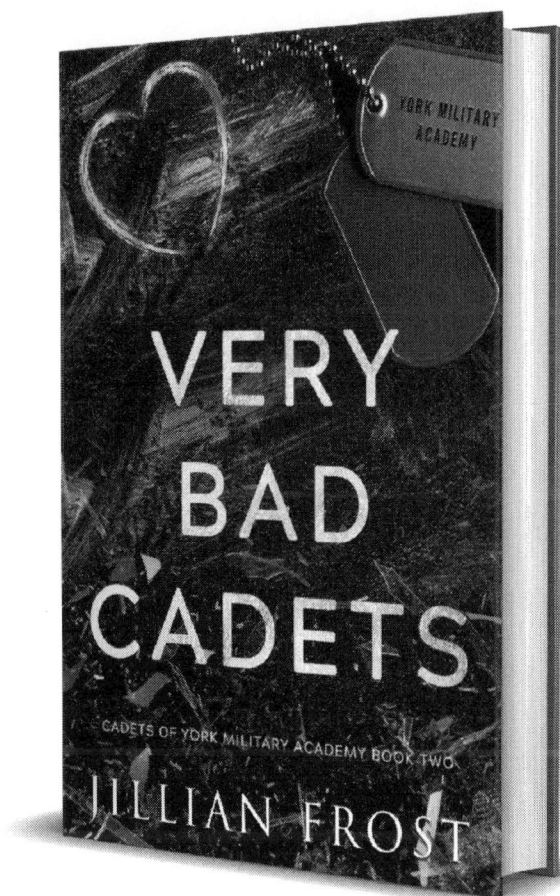

Read the conclusion to Grace's story with her cadets.

**Learn more about the series at
JillianFrost.com**

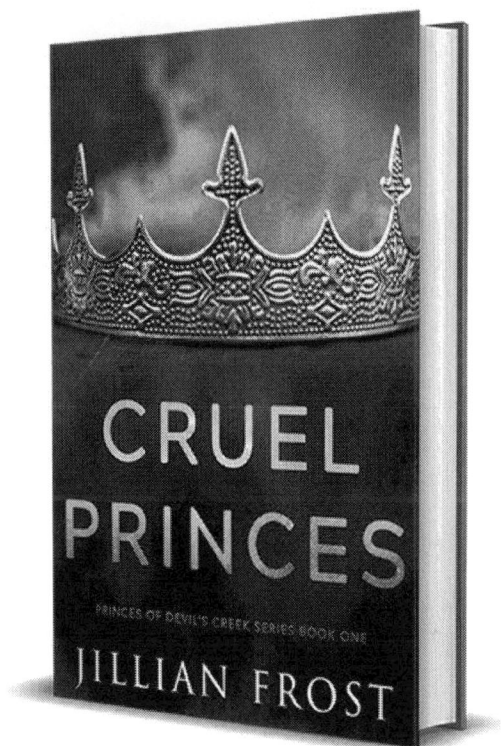

Meet the Salvatore brothers and the Queen of The Devil's Knights.

Learn more about the series at JillianFrost.com

Are you a Frost Fangirl?

Get access to exclusive bonus scenes and Jillian Frost books you can't find anywhere else. You'll also be the first to know about new releases and giveaways.

Join the team at JillianFrost.com

Get to know Jillian Frost

Watch Jillian's latest videos on TikTok
@jillianfrostbooks

Get sneak peeks and an all-access pass to Jillian on
Facebook when you join her private reader's group
called Frost's Fangirls

Check out the latest teasers and pretty pictures on
Jillian's Instagram @jillianfrostbooks

Also by Jillian Frost

Princes of Devil's Creek Series

Cruel Princes

Vicious Queen

Savage Knights

Cadets of York Military Academy Series

Filthy Rich Cadets

Very Bad Cadets

For a complete list of books, visit JillianFrost.com.

About the Author

Jillian Frost is a dark romance author who believes even the villain deserves a happily ever after. She loves writing twisted suspense plots about dangerous but redeemable antiheroes. When she's not plotting all the ways to disrupt the lives of her characters, you can usually find Jillian by the pool, soaking up the Florida sunshine.

Manufactured by Amazon.ca
Bolton, ON